Praise for *F*

High school is not the easiest place to be an individual especially if you don't fit into the MTV generation's mold of the perfect body. *Fourteen* explores a brief glimpse into the world of a teenage girl that is not a size two, and because of this, she is ridiculed and ostracized by her peers. Her main goal at the beginning of the story is to "get through high school."

I would dare to say that the majority of the population has felt these insecurities at some point in their lives, and the rest of those who say they haven't are lying. It has been years since I attended high school; however, reading about Anna's plight brings back emotions that I have not felt in a long time.

C.M. Smith's writing is excellent, and the raw emotions of all her characters suck you into the story and leave you absolutely breathless at times. It is rare when can pull you in so much that you identify with everything each of the characters experience and make you feel as if the story is about you. When it happens, it's magical.

Fourteen is an experience for every reader—whether you were the one being bullied or you were the bully. There are life lessons we can all enjoy in this story, and I will not soon forget.

J Pedroza- The ReviewLounge

C.M. Smith

Fourteen

The Writer's Coffee Shop
Publishing House

First published by The Writer's Coffee Shop, 2011

The Writer's Coffee Shop
(Australia)   PO Box 2013 Hornsby Westfield NSW 1635
(USA)   PO Box 2116 Waxahachie TX 75168

Paperback ISBN- 978-1-61213-042-2
E-book ISBN- 978-1-61213-043-9

A CIP catalogue record for this book is available from the US Congress Library.

Cover image by: Jomann
Cover design by: Jennifer McGuire

www.thewriterscoffeeshop.com/csmith

About the Author

C.M. Smith doesn't remember ever not writing or reading. Like so many young children, her mother and grandmother read to her every night before she went to bed and before long, she'd decided to try her hand at writing something of her own. She has spent the better part of her life writing short stories or novels that she's only shared with a few select people. She finally took the plunge in late 2009 and decided to publish her first novel, *Fourteen*.

C.M. lives in upstate New York with her family.

Acknowledgments

First, I'd like to thank everyone that has this book in their hands for reading. I want to say that a size fourteen, in my opinion, is not a big or bad size. I'm a size fourteen, in fact, and I happen to think that there's nothing wrong with that. I hope that this was evident in my writing, as it was never my intention to imply fourteen was anything other than a size. I chose that size simply because I was close to it and was able to relate to that more—not for any other reason.

I hope that everyone who has read this has been able to realize that you're all beautiful, no matter what size you may be. Never let anyone tell you differently.

Thank you for reading,
C.M. Smith

C.M. Smith

Chapter One

Fourteen.

It was not a bad number.

It was not that great, either.

It used to be an eighteen; so really, a fourteen was pretty damn good compared to what it was a few months ago.

It was still a big number, and staring at the jeans lying on my bed, they looked pretty damn big, too.

I wasn't thin. I was moderately pretty and had more personality in my left toe than most of the girls at school had at all.

Arianna Weller was my name, synonymous with size fourteen, and no one was able to see past *that*. At least, the guys couldn't. Most of the popular girls couldn't, either.

Christina did, and she was popular. It continually surprised me when she hung out with me or sat with me during lunch. Her boyfriend—third baseman, Vince—was one of the few guys that actually didn't make fun of me behind my back and would freely walk up and talk to me if he saw me in the hallway. Kyle Mahon would sometimes, too, but that was only if no one else was around to rag on him about it.

I didn't even consider a size fourteen that big, to be honest. Marilyn Monroe had been a size fourteen, and she'd been considered a beautiful woman. Of course, that was many years ago, and society's image of a beautiful woman had severely changed since then. I've learned that if you're above a size four, you have to have some severe personality quirks to fit in —be a class clown, or you just have to be lucky enough to be confident with who you are and what you look like. I am neither of those things.

Fourteen

I didn't have many friends. I had acquaintances that I talked to during the day, but none of them were anything near a friend for me. It was by choice more than anything. I'd gotten used to being picked on and put down or betrayed by people I thought were friends. They either told secrets that I'd rather they kept—well, secret—or they just distanced themselves from me because I was no longer cool enough for them.

I didn't know what it was about me that pushed people away. I didn't do it on purpose, but it happened more often than not. Maybe I was just too . . . me. Though I often thought about compromising to fit in, to be "enough" for them, I just couldn't.

I'd gotten used to not being good enough, and at the end of the previous school year, I'd done myself a favor. I'd kept myself as far away from as many people as possible in this tiny shithole. I was off to college next year—New York University—and if I could get through my last year at Collins Point High as peacefully as possible, I'd be a very happy person. The fewer attachments I had when I left, the easier it would be to move somewhere and start over.

I was all about starting over.

Shuffling my feet against the carpet, I grabbed the jeans from my bed, sliding them on over my legs and wiggling into them, then buttoning them and grabbing my long-sleeved red sweater and pulling it on over my head. I sighed in disappointment as I looked down at the small roll of flesh around my waist. I walked over to my dresser and ran a brush through my shoulder-length dark brown hair a few times, briefly looking at my reflection in the small mirror propped against the wall. I'd never found myself all that attractive. I had blue eyes, my nose wasn't huge, but it was bigger than I appreciated, and my face was too round for my liking. I had a bit of a double chin and my collarbones weren't visible like most of the girls in school. I grabbed my book bag from the floor and slung it over my shoulder. I walked to the door, flipped off the lights, and went down the stairs.

My father, Bruce Weller, was a lawyer and had left for work long before I was out of bed. I was thankful for the peace and quiet each morning. I was not a morning person by any means, and Dad most certainly was. We didn't talk much as it was, but having to deal with his chipper—well, chipper compared to me—attitude first thing in the morning had never been something I enjoyed.

It was just the two of us after my mom died in a car accident five years ago. I was thirteen years old, and my father has spent those last five years, avoiding me and doing the bare minimum when it came to parenting. Yes, he was there when I needed him for school-related functions, and I knew that he loved me; he just had a funny way of showing it sometimes.

His days were spent at his office. I couldn't imagine he did much of anything while he was there. Though he earned enough to keep us living comfortably, Collins Point wasn't exactly a hotbed of illegal activity, and I couldn't imagine many people needed his services. When he wasn't at the office, he was either falling asleep in front of the Discovery Channel, or finding unnecessary repairs around the house to make worse. Mr. Fix-It he was not.

I grabbed a granola bar from the cabinet, shoved it into the front of my bag, and grabbed my keys as I slid on my sneakers. I locked the front door and pulled it closed, listening for it to slam shut as I made my way down the steps and into the light rain.

I jumped over a puddle on my way to my car, wrenched open the door, and threw my bag onto the passenger seat as I plopped into the driver's seat. Then I slammed the door shut and smoothed my hands over my hair just in case, shoving the key in the ignition and backing out of the driveway.

I pulled into the school parking lot ten minutes later, keeping my eyes on the pavement in front of me as I drove to my favorite parking spot. I felt the familiar stares and sucked in a deep breath, shoving my car into park and grabbing my bag.

My car was an ancient Dodge Neon that made more noise than your average motorboat, and I was the weird quiet girl. I was thankful that I didn't need glasses or braces because my life would be over if I had to deal with *that* on top of weighing more than one hundred and ten pounds.

Stepping out of the car, I slung my bag over my shoulder, pocketing my keys and slamming the door. I kept my head down as I walked behind Brittany Feldman, Steve Forrester, Adam Leveque, and Grace Alcott to the front of the school. Thankfully, they didn't pay me any notice, and I made it to my locker in peace as I breathed a sigh of relief, twirling the lock and yanking open the door.

I stuffed my bag into my locker and grabbed the books I would need for my first period human physiology class. When I got to class, I flipped through the back pages of my notebook for the homework I'd stored there the night before. When I didn't find it, I groaned and slammed my book shut. By the time I got back to my locker, groups of students had formed around the area, so I kept my eyes on the floor. It was always quiet over in this corner; everyone else who had nearby lockers usually went to talk to one of their friends on the other end of the hallway, and for that, I was thankful. The less people I had to interact with, the better.

I'd never been a very social person. I was shy and being in a school as small as this for my entire life had left me with no self-esteem whatsoever, because I'd never been thin or outgoing, and they took great pleasure in reminding me daily.

I could get pissed off. Sometimes I had fantasies about whining to my father and asking him to find a just reason to sue any of their parents, but adding fuel to an already hot fire would only make things worse for me.

I just wanted to get through my senior year with as much dignity as I possibly could, and pissing off everyone in my way wouldn't help.

I rummaged around in my book bag, and got nervous when I came up empty. The warning bell rang, and I yanked my books out of my locker. Balancing them in one hand, I searched the bottom and hoped and prayed that it had gotten pushed to the back when I'd left yesterday. When that didn't work, I huffed and shoved the books back into the locker, ripping open the front pocket of my bag and searching through that as well.

I finally found it, breathed a sigh of relief, and held it tightly in my hand as I slammed my locker shut. The only other person in the hallway now was Evan Drake, his usually neat brown hair sticking up all over the place as he attempted to push his book bag into the locker already crowded with his baseball gear.

Apparently he'd gotten in late.

"Son of a bitch," he whispered, pulling on the strap of his book bag and yanking back.

Papers flew out of the open top and fell effortlessly to the ground. He stood there, his chest heaving and his breathing audible as he narrowed his eyes at the mess he'd made.

Evan Drake was one of the guys that tormented me on a daily basis. He was gorgeous and he knew it, which made it ten times worse. His face was flawless and always clear of any acne, and his jawline and cheekbones were works of art. Square, chiseled, and made more for a male model than a high school student. He dated whomever he wanted and never looked twice at anyone that wasn't on the cheerleading squad or within the realm of popularity. He was "Mr. Perfect," according to everyone in the entire school, and I'd harbored a major crush for as long as I could remember. Unfortunately, he was anything but "Mr. Perfect," and it was something that I struggled with daily.

I hated myself for it, because I didn't understand it. He tormented me and said the most horrible things but there had been a time when we were much younger—barely out of kindergarten, I think—when we were playmates. Our mothers had been friendly with each other and had set up play dates for us while they spent the afternoon on the back porch of his home. We spent that time running around his backyard, pretending that we were pirates with swords or we were Steve Irwin prodigies as we inspected whatever small animal that dared to come our way. Then middle school happened, and he got more involved with sports and discovered that I wasn't the ideal shape his friends preferred in their girl choices. We stopped talking, and for a while, I was merely ignored by him and his new friends. Then society seemed to take over and because Evan had a short past with me, I'd become the main target of their ridicule. Regardless, I was always hoping that there was still a piece of the younger Evan I used to play with hanging around in him somewhere. He was always kind to his younger sister, and he seemed like a completely different person when I saw him out with his parents. When he was with his family, he was carefree, always laughing, and he didn't have that superior air around him, and that gave me something really close to hope. There had to be something left of his younger self if he could act like that with his family, right?

Either way, I'd be out of this place in a few months and able to forget all about Evan Drake and the way I didn't want to feel for him. I repeated my mantra, *I could start over,* and that was all I really wanted.

But right now, as I watched him breathing hard and glaring at the mess on the floor, all I felt was sympathy for him. He'd obviously had a bad morning, and it was only getting worse, it seemed.

I folded my homework in half and started toward him. His eyes snapped to me, and he narrowed them even further. I wordlessly bent down, sticking my homework under my arm and reaching for the papers scattered on the floor.

"What the fuck are you doing?"

"Helping you," I said.

My voice was quiet and came out as a squeak, my nerves showing through as I tapped papers together on the floor before crawling over to get some more.

"I don't *need* your help."

"Sure doesn't seem that way."

"Go the fuck away, Arianna. I can handle picking up my own damn papers."

My heart twisted, and I clenched my teeth together, ignoring him as I continued to pick up the papers covered with his neat handwriting. I was at his feet by that point, my heart hammering against my ribs, when he bent down. He grabbed my wrist, hard, and I looked up at him.

Fear shot through me when I met his cold eyes, and I barely contained a yelp as he tightened his hand around my wrist. I felt tears spring to my eyes.

"I said," he said, his voice low and rough, "to go the fuck away."

I dropped his papers, and he dropped my wrist as I fell backward, cradling my wrist to my chest and biting down on my trembling lip. Looking down, I saw the red imprints of his fingers and knew I would have a bruise there by the end of the day. I placed my feet flat on the floor, pushed myself away from him, and did my best to control the tears as I grabbed my homework from underneath my arm and placed my uninjured hand flat on the floor.

"Sorry," I whispered and pushed myself to stand up, keeping my eyes on the floor.

"You should be. What right do you think you have to just touch my things?"

"I was only trying to help."

"Yeah? Well, don't. If I should ever need you for any fucking thing," he scoffed, "you'll be the first to know."

I closed my eyes, and waited. He slammed the locker door shut a few moments later, and I listened to his footsteps as they faded down the hallway. I sucked in a few deep breaths and brought my wrist up to inspect the marks that were getting redder, letting a small shuddering sob escape my chest before I sucked it in and blinked rapidly to get rid of the tears. The bell rang, signifying that first period was about to start, and I walked back to the classroom. I kept my head down as I walked to my table, moved around the person sitting in the chair next to mine, and plopped down.

"Oh, for fuck's sake," a voice said from beside me.

I looked over to see Evan staring at me in disgust. I looked away and over to where he normally sat. Brittany and Grace were now seated at his table, snickering and pointing at me. He turned and glared at them, flipping his middle finger at Brittany when she blew him a kiss.

"All right! Good morning, class," Mr. Streeter said, clapping his hands to get everyone's attention.

I looked up toward the front, keeping my injured wrist in my lap and nervously twirling a lock of my hair with my free hand.

Just another day, Anna. One more day closer to graduation and getting the hell out of here. It's just one more day. Remember—starting over.

"Look to the person you're sitting next to," Mr. Streeter said, holding his hands up in the air, palms facing out.

"Do I have to?" Evan asked, leaning forward and resting his head in his hand.

Snickers erupted throughout the room, and I looked down at my lap as tears flooded my eyes.

"This will be your partner for the project that I'm assigning."

"You've gotta be kidding me!" Evan exclaimed, slamming his fist down on the table. I jumped, wanting to crawl into a hole when everyone laughed at me. "You want me to deal with *this*?"

"You will or you fail," Mr. Streeter deadpanned, turning his back on us and walking to the chalkboard.

I kept my eyes on my notebook for the rest of class, barely hearing anything as the teacher told us the requirements for the upcoming science fair. I listened to Evan grumble about the whole situation the entire time. My jaw ached with the effort I used to keep the tears from falling.

I set my injured wrist on the table at one point and shifted uneasily on the uncomfortable stool. I heard Evan take a sharp breath, and I glanced over at him, noticing his eyes were focused on the marks that were rapidly becoming bruises. I pulled it back to my lap and stopped trying to get comfortable after that. I didn't know what his expression meant, but if he wanted to hurt me again, I didn't want to give him any more ammunition.

The bell finally rang, and I was quick to gather my things, minding my wrist as I juggled the books in my arms.

"Arianna, I'm—" Evan began, his voice low and quiet.

"I'm sorry that you're stuck with me, Evan," I said, cutting him off. "I'll do all the work by myself if you prefer."

"No, I just wanted to make sure—"

"I'll be sure to put your name on it as well. I've got it covered." I squeezed by him. I walked out of the room and hurried to my locker, grabbing the books I'd need for my next class. The day had started out badly enough, and I *really* didn't want it to get any worse.

~*~

I trudged up the porch steps to the house, my book bag trailing behind me and bouncing against the steps as I walked.

My dad wasn't home yet. He was almost never here when I got home, and for the first time in a long time, I was thankful that he wasn't. I didn't mind being alone in the mornings, but I really hated coming home to an empty house after school. I usually wanted someone to talk to because going through the day by myself only made me lonely.

Today, however, I welcomed the silence.

My wrist throbbed, and as the day went on, I noticed it was even a little puffy. I'd gone to the nurse in between third and fourth period to get an ice pack, stating that I'd fallen down and landed on it the wrong way. During lunch, I'd bought orange juice and set my wrist on the bottle the entire time. No one sat with me—Christina and Vince were nowhere to be found, and I suspected that they were breaking in the backseat of his newly-acquired Honda—so I didn't have to worry about explaining anything. What could I say? I didn't want to get Christina and Vince started. Upsetting the balance of the sports in this school would not bode well, and no one else would believe that perfect Evan Drake had stooped so low to actually *touch* me. It wouldn't make a difference if they'd seen it with their own two eyes.

After grabbing an ice pack from the freezer, I made it into my room and set my book bag down by my nightstand. Plopping down onto my bed, I cradled my wrist and the ice pack in my hand and rested it in my lap. It was definitely bruised and still a little puffy, but it wasn't as bad as it could've been.

I felt the sting of tears and leaned forward, resting my feet on the bed frame and burying my face in my knees. I crushed my wrist against my chest and wrapped my other arm around my legs. My tears fell and my sobs filled my empty room.

I wasn't a bad person. I'd done my best to be nice to everyone in our school, and they just didn't care. They were so concerned with the way I looked that it didn't matter to them if we liked the same things. It didn't matter if our favorite bands were the same, or if we felt the same way about something that we'd heard on the news. I wasn't thin, and I wasn't popular, so I had to become their target.

It wasn't as if I was the only heavy person in our school. Yes, it was a small school, but not everyone was as thin as their group was.

I didn't know how long I sat there crying, my tears and sobs a product of everything that had gone wrong during the day. I heard a series of loud knocks on the door downstairs, but I ignored it, hoping that whoever it was would go away. I wiped the tears from my face and did my best to get my breathing under control.

But the mystery visitor continued to pound on the door. I finally huffed with annoyance. Keeping my wrist close to my chest and placing the ice pack on my bed, I rubbed the heel of my other hand in my eye as I walked down the stairs. I yanked open the door and caught my breath when I saw Evan standing there.

"C . . . can I help you?" I asked, my voice trembling as I gripped the doorknob tightly and wished that my father were home.

Not that he would do anything about it, anyway. He adored Evan's father and the rest of his damn family. But at least he would've been there, and Evan wouldn't have been able to—well, I didn't know what he wanted to do. But either way, he wouldn't have been able to do it with my father home.

Evan shifted uncomfortably, shuffling his feet on the blue welcome mat that had been there ever since I could remember. He gripped the strap of his book bag, looked at his feet, and shrugging one shoulder.

"I just thought that maybe we should start on this thing. The sooner we do, the sooner we get it finished."

The sooner you get to stop associating with me.

"I told you that I'd take care of it."

"I'm just as capable as you are, Arianna," he snapped, looking up at me and glaring. "I'm not a fucking idiot."

I looked down at my feet.

"You know *nothing* about me." He sounded on edge.

I instantly shied away from him, shielding myself behind the door, and tried to control the sudden flow of tears.

"I just thought that . . . since you obviously don't want to work with me, I could . . . you wouldn't have to . . ." My voice caught, and I hid my face from him, working myself completely behind the door. "Can we not start this tonight?"

Fourteen

"Shit, Arianna, I want to . . ." He slapped the doorjamb, and I flinched, my hand tightening on the doorknob. "Let me see your wrist."

"It's fine. Please leave."

"It's *not* fine because you're still being careful with it. Let me see it."

"Why? You want to make it worse?"

"No!" he shouted, and I needed that hole to open up and swallow me now. He huffed out a breath and seemed to stand up a little straighter. "I just want to see it."

"I don't—"

His shoulders slumped, and his Adam's apple bobbed in his throat as he swallowed hard.

"Just let me see your wrist. I won't hurt you."

I didn't move, my entire body shaking as I stood on the other side of the door, wondering why it was so important. It was easy to see that I was of no importance to him, so why was he so adamant about seeing my wrist? What did he want to gain from it? He said that he wouldn't hurt me, but I never believed he'd do it the first time—why would I willingly hand over the same part of my body he'd already bruised?

"Arianna, I promise that I won't hurt you again. I just want to see it." His voice wasn't as hard as it had been before.

"Why?" I asked, my voice trembling.

"I want to make sure it's okay."

"It's fine. I told you that."

"And I told you that it wasn't."

"Will you leave then?"

"If you want me to."

"I do."

"Then I'll leave after you show it to me."

I cautiously stepped out from behind the door and pulled it open a little more.

"Can I come in?"

"Why?"

"It's getting dark out here. I won't be able to see very well."

I stepped back as he pushed the door open and walked in, closing it behind him and dropping his book bag to the floor. I held my arm out to him, and my heart thundered in my chest as he gently grabbed my hand. He flexed my wrist back and forth, his face blank, but that was before he pressed two fingers against the bruises. I cried out and immediately pulled my hand back from him, holding it to my chest. He stared at my wrist, reaching up to rub the back of his neck.

"Will you put it against your other one?" he asked, finally meeting my eyes again.

"For what?"

"Will you just do it?" he snapped.

I flinched, and his face fell.

"You should uh . . . you should put some ice on it," he said. "It won't be so puffy tomorrow if you do."

I was at a loss for words. He actually seemed concerned.

"Okay."

"I guess I'll go now," he mumbled, reaching down and grabbing his book bag. "We should figure out something to do for the science fair, maybe tomorrow in class or something."

"Yeah." I looked down at my feet.

He hesitated, and I looked up at him. He hastily pulled the door open and walked out. I closed the door behind him, locked it, and walked back up to my room.

Maybe there wasn't anything more to Evan Drake after all. Maybe I just wished that there were because I really wanted there to be something more underneath the shallowness and the pretty face. Maybe I just wanted someone like him to be a good person because there weren't very many at my school.

Maybe I just needed to stop hoping for things. It never got me anything but hurt, and I was *really* tired of hurting.

Dad came home around six-thirty, explaining that they'd gotten a huge case and he hadn't been able to call. He handed me the food he'd bought on the way home and then sat down in front of the television for the rest of the night while I did my homework.

He didn't ask about the ice pack I held to my wrist. He didn't ask how my day was. He didn't ask if everything was okay when it clearly was not.

I wished I could be as invisible to my classmates like I was to my father sometimes. It would make my life a hell of a lot easier in the long run.

Chapter Two

I kept my head down, and my hands shoved into the pocket of my hoodie as I made my way up to the front of the school the next morning. When I woke up, the last person I wanted to see and deal with in my first period class was Evan. So I'd spent most of the morning, trying to convince myself that, yes, I did have to go to school today.

I'd decided last night that I was done liking him. Whatever I'd witnessed when he was with his family clearly was only for show, there wasn't any part left of the little boy I used to play with, and there was nothing more to him. I was the idiot that had wasted entirely too much of my life, wishing that he'd open his eyes and see that I was an actual person.

Something everyone else failed to see because I didn't participate in sports or any extracurricular activities, and didn't offer up the answers in class unless the teacher called on me.

I made it into the school, raced to my locker, shoved my things inside, and grabbed my books before walking to the classroom. I had made sure that everything was where it was supposed to be before I left the house so that I could avoid a scene like what had happened yesterday. The less time I spent alone, the less opportunities Evan had of bruising my other wrist.

It wasn't puffy anymore, but there were still bruises, and it was difficult to shower the night before. I'd managed to hit it on every surface in the bathroom, and by the time I crawled into bed, it was throbbing again.

On top of that, I'd had dreams about him. In one, he was pushing me off a cliff and laughing maniacally as I fell. In another one, he was taking care of me and making sure that my wrist was okay. He'd actually—I sighed and plopped down onto the stool, leaning forward, and burying my face in my arms—he'd actually kissed it and apologized to me, saying that he didn't mean it, that he was just having a bit of a rough morning, that he'd never meant to hurt me, and then he'd kissed *me*.

I guess that's why they're called dreams; the most impossible things can happen when you're lost in your own head.

I tensed when I heard the stool next to me slide against the linoleum floor, and I slowly sat up and stared straight ahead at the chalkboard. I placed my hands in my lap and looked at the clock on the wall. It wasn't hard to recognize *him* sitting next to me, even from the corner of my eye.

It wasn't even time for the warning bell to ring yet. What was he doing here? He had a ton of minions waiting with baited breath for the next word out of his mouth, and he was in his first period class before anyone else? I couldn't believe that he'd come in here just to speak to me and briefly wondered what excuse he had made to the aforementioned minions so that they wouldn't follow him in here.

When he said nothing, I flipped open my human physiology book and scanned the pages so I had something to do. Just sitting here with him was like a neon sign that said, *She's pathetic! She thinks Evan Drake would actually talk to her if she just sat here!* Even though I didn't.

I didn't even *want* him to talk to me. I didn't want to be his partner. I didn't want to talk to him ever again. He wasn't the person I thought he could still be, and I'd seriously fooled myself into thinking anything of the sort. I was unbelievably mad and frustrated with myself. I had always believed that I was smarter than the other girls that I'd heard stories about. It turned out that I was just as foolish as the rest of them.

"How are you this morning, Arianna?" he whispered.

"Peachy."

"How's your wrist?"

I switched arms, immediately hiding the hurt one underneath the desk and draping it across my lap as I stared down at a diagram of a frog.

"It's fine," I said, flipping through the pages.

"Can I see it?"

"You saw it last night." I looked over at him before looking back down at my book. "You don't need to see it today, too."

"Look, I get it. I fucked up yesterday. I'm trying to be nice, Arianna."

"Why now? I've known you my entire life, and it takes something like you bruising me to make you talk to me again? Why couldn't you have tried to be nice to me before?"

I looked over at him when he failed to answer and found him staring down at our lab table, his hands braced against the edge as if he needed something to keep him upright. I opened my mouth to say something else, snapped it shut, and looked back up at the chalkboard. He didn't have an answer, and I had nothing left to say.

"What did you want to do for this stupid thing, anyway?" he finally grumbled a few moments later.

"I was looking online last night and found something about a lie detector test. I thought it seemed interesting," I said, shrugging.

"Fine. Great." He slid his stool back and stood up. "Did you print it out?"

"Yeah," I said, and then listened as his footsteps echoed in the empty room as he walked out. I slumped over my books, crossing my arms and burying my head in them again.

Just a few more weeks and I wouldn't have to talk to him about anything ever again. We'd finish this project and go back to our separate lives, pretending that nothing had ever happened. And I could pretend that everything he hadn't said to me hadn't hurt like a bitch.

~*~

"So . . . did you want to come over tonight to work on this some more?" I asked, closing my book and stuffing the information I had printed out back into my folder.

"I have practice tonight."

"Okay." I stacked my books and placed my arms on the table, surrounding them, staring at the back of Steve Forrester's head as I waited for the bell to ring.

We'd been given the entire period to get our projects sorted out so that we could get started on them. The science fair was in three weeks, and while not every class would be dedicated to the project, a good portion of our future ones would be. We would still have tests to take and other homework to do, so working outside of class was crucial.

Neither of us was very happy about that. "I'll get started on it tonight, then, and fill you in during class tomorrow."

"I can come over after practice," he said in a low voice, and I stared at him as he looked around the room as if to see if anyone had heard him.

"Whatever you want to do, Evan."

"We finish around five. I'll be there around five forty-five."

"Sounds good." I stared straight ahead and looked away from Steve as he turned around to talk to Evan.

"How's it going, dude?"

Evan shrugged.

"Has she tried to like . . . molest you or anything? It's not like she's ever had any action."

I clenched my jaw and looked out the window, placing one arm in my lap and resting my chin in the other.

"No, she hasn't. I'm keeping my distance."

"Don't let her get too close. She'll sit on you. Probably crush your entire body while she's at it, too."

I sucked in a deep breath and grabbed my books. I slid off the stool, walked up to the front of the room, and leaned over Mr. Streeter's desk as I waited for him to look up at me.

"Can I leave a little early, Mr. Streeter?" I asked, embarrassed when my voice shook.

I had never cried during school before. Things rarely happened that hurt so badly that I couldn't wait until I got home at the end of the day. I had dealt with Steve Forrester and Grace Alcott screaming out fat jokes without crying. I had dealt with Brittany Feldman pointing and laughing at me as I changed for gym class without crying. But in the past two days and all thanks to Evan Drake, it was like I did nothing *but* cry. It was just one more thing that kept me infuriated with myself.

"Is everything all right, Anna?" he asked, his eyes darting from me to what I assumed was my lab desk.

"Yes, I just have . . . um . . . can I please go?"

"I suppose so. Feel better."

I offered him a shaky smile in thanks before walking out of the room and to my locker, breathing deeply as I switched out my books for my next class.

What had I ever done to any of them to make them say things like that about me?

~*~

I scribbled a note to my father just in case he came home early and grabbed my keys and iPod from the table. I placed the ear buds into my ears, pushed *play* on my iPod, and stuffed it and my keys into my pocket before I locked the door and walked out of the house. I jumped down the stairs, taking a deep breath and spreading my legs, leaning over and stretching before standing back up and jogging down the road.

I tried to run at least three times a week. Not only had I shed two sizes since I'd started, but it had also helped clear my mind a little. And after a day like today, a little clarity was something I definitely needed.

For the rest of the day, I had managed to keep my emotions in check. It also helped that Evan wasn't in any of my other classes and all I had to deal with was Brittany and Grace, laughing and pointing and making snide comments like they always did. I had learned early on how to block them out, and couldn't understand why I couldn't do the same thing with Evan.

Why did *his* insults hurt so much more than anyone else's jibes? He wasn't saying anything new; in fact, it was all getting pretty old. Honestly, I'd stopped caring and listening to them for the most part.

What was it about him that just made it hurt so much? My self-esteem had always been low, but he'd completely destroyed any I might have had left. I get that I was nothing to him; I was nothing to any of them. But I'd never seen the use in insulting the people I didn't truly know anything about, and I didn't understand why they thought they had a right to do the same to me.

I jogged by Brittany Feldman's grandmother's house, briefly wondering if she knew about how much of a cruel bitch her granddaughter really was.

I concentrated on the music flowing from my ear buds as I continued down the street.

It didn't matter. Nothing mattered right now. I hadn't had a bad day at school. I hadn't had to deal with anyone that couldn't come up with an original joke. I hadn't come home to an empty house and a heavy heart. And I most certainly hadn't cried because Evan Drake had agreed with Steve Forrester this morning.

They didn't know me. They didn't know anything that was going on in my life, so them making comments like that and saying those things were not important. It didn't matter. *They* didn't matter to *me*.

Just a few more months. Graduation isn't that far away, and NYU is waiting for me. I can deal with this shit for just a few more months.

I turned around just before the street Steve Forrester lived on and jogged back home. I walked up the porch steps, once again, greeted with an empty house. After setting my iPod and keys on the small end table by the door, I walked into the kitchen, crumpled up the note to Dad, and threw it away.

I looked at the clock on the microwave—ten past five. I had plenty of time to take a shower before Evan showed up.

If he showed up.

Rolling my eyes and sighing, I made it up the stairs and into the bathroom. After stripping, I turned and looked in the mirror and placed my palms on my stomach. I spread my hands, stretching my skin until it was flat, and turned sideways. My stomach was falsely flat now, but my butt still stuck out more than what was considered "ideal" for a teenage girl. My arms were flabby as well, and I wore long-sleeved shirts no matter what the weather, just to cover them up. My thighs were thick and at eighteen years old, I had cellulite regardless how much I ran. The only decently thin part of my body was my calves. I did this every time I took a shower, imagining how I'd look if I were skinny. It only made me feel disappointed, disgusted with myself, and upset. Today, I just didn't care. Today, I accepted that I looked like this, and while I wouldn't be a beauty queen at any point in my life, this was me. Right now, that was enough.

I dropped my hands from my stomach and turned from the mirror, leaning down and testing the water temperature before I pulled on the lever and hopped in.

Afterward, I stepped out, grabbed a towel from the cabinet underneath the sink, and wrapped it around me. I grabbed my clothes from the floor and kicked my shoes out into the hallway as I walked into my bedroom. Tossing my clothes into the wicker basket by my closet, I pulled on a pair of sweatpants and long-sleeved back shirt. With a towel, I dried my hair, ran my brush through it, and walked downstairs in time to hear a knock at the door.

Pulling at the ends of my shirt, I took a deep breath to prepare myself and pulled open the door. His hair was wet, either from sweat or a shower, and he was dressed in the same clothes he'd worn to school—a white t-shirt, black zip-up hoodie, and a pair of dark blue jeans.

"Hi." He shifted his book bag on his shoulder and looked down at his feet.

"Hi," I said, stepping out of the way and letting him in.

I closed the door, skirted around him and started toward the kitchen.

"We can work in here, I guess," I said, snatching my bag from the floor, walking into the kitchen, and setting it in a chair before going over to the refrigerator. "Would you like anything to drink?"

"What do you have?"

I looked behind me to see that he was standing at the table, his bag on the floor and his hands resting on the chair he stood behind.

"Water, iced tea, and soda."

"Water."

I closed the refrigerator after grabbing a bottle of iced tea for myself. I placed his drink in front of him, moved my book bag from the chair, and sat down. I set my iced tea down and unzipped my bag, grabbing my human physiology textbook and notebook and setting it on the table.

"We need at least ten volunteers," I said, flipping open my notebook and handing him the project information. "Since I don't know ten people, I guess that's your job."

"You know ten people, Arianna," he said, grabbing the paper and reading over it.

"Would any of them be willing to help me out?" I asked dryly, looking up at him and tilting my head to the side.

He looked at me over the edge of the paper, his eyes trailing back to the words in front of him.

"I was thinking that we should try it out on each other first." I played with the edges of my notebook, keeping my eyes on the middle of the table. "So that we know what we're looking for."

"All right," he agreed. "We have to write a paper, too. Right?"

"Yes. I can do that if you'll get the volunteers."

"I can handle the responsibility of writing a paper, Arianna."

He glared at me, and I instinctively slid down in my seat.

"I'm just trying to make this *easier* for you. The less you have to deal with me, the better, right?" I said with a voice laced with sarcasm as I gave him a fake smile that bordered on a sneer.

"It's a joint project," he said through his teeth. "I'm capable of doing more than finding fucking volunteers for this shit."

I held my hands up in mock surrender and feigned innocence. "Geez. Didn't mean to offend. Sor-ry."

"We can split the paper," he said, snapping the pages down on the table. "We'll work on it together."

He bent over to open his bag, pulling out a notebook and a pen of his own. He flipped it open to a blank page and tapped his pen on it. I did the same, pulling a pen out from my bag and immediately drew the chart that I'd seen on the webpage.

The whole idea of this type of lie detector test had to do with the way the body reacted when someone was lying. For example, when people lied, they usually tensed up, their facial expression changed, their voice changed in pitch and their entire body stiffened. When people told the truth, they were more relaxed and easygoing. The website had said to make a chart with three truths on one side and three lies on the other. One person had to hold out his arm while the other pushed down on it as he told either a lie or the truth, and it was the asker's job to watch for the rest of the signs. The way the body reacted determined whether the person was telling the truth or not.

"Do you want to go first?" I asked keeping my eyes centered on the page as I wrote what I liked.

Running. Classical music. Reading.

"I guess so."

I wrote my dislikes in the second column.

High school. Mosquitoes. Sun.

I looked up to see that he was writing things down as well, briefly wondering what he most disliked about his life. He seemed to have everything.

"Done," he said, setting the pen down on his notebook and looking over at me.

We both stood.

"We should do this on the stairs. I have to be taller than you."

He turned on his heel, walking in the direction of the front door. He stopped and I walked in front of him, standing on the second step and waiting for him to stand in front of me. He stuck his arm out, and I placed my hand on his wrist and looked at his shoulder.

"We should probably do a few control questions, so that we both know what to expect."

"What should I start with? Lie or truth?"

"Whatever you'd like."

He pursed his lips and twisted them to the side. I hated the way my heart skipped a beat and the way I wanted to smile. He looked like the boy I used to know when he did that. Evan's face smoothed out after a moment, and he shifted his weight on his feet, standing up straight.

"My name is Evan Drake."

I studied him as I slowly pushed down on his arm, noting the way his face was completely relaxed, and it took no effort whatsoever to push his arm to his side.

"That was the truth," I said, more to help myself remember the little details than anything else.

"I know my own damn name."

"No, I know. I just . . ." I shook my head to clear it. "Never mind."

He rolled his eyes, stuck his arm out once more, and I replaced my hand on his wrist.

"I am a geek."

I repressed the urge to roll my eyes as I pushed down on his arm, noting the way his eyes tightened at the corners and his lips pursed slightly. It was harder to push his arm down and even his shoulders seemed rigid.

"Great," I mumbled, letting go of his wrist and standing up straight once more.

"Truth or lie?" he challenged.

"Lie," I said through my teeth.

He nodded, satisfied, and stuck out his arm again. "Do you have enough of a grip on what to expect now or should we continue on with the controls?"

"I have all the information I need from you. You might have to do the same to me when it comes to that."

The smug look on his face fell, and he scowled at me, sticking his arm out once more. I felt a mild satisfaction from ruffling his feathers and put my hand on his wrist again.

"Whenever you're ready."

He shifted on his feet.

"I love my car."

I slowly pushed down on his arm as he said it, checking all the factors of his face that I'd picked out before.

Truth.

He raised his arm again. "I think you're beautiful."

I studied his face, feeling the tears build up in the back of my throat. His lips were stretched into a thin line, his arm was nearly impossible to push down, and every inch of him was rigid.

Lie.

"I forgot my notebook." I managed to say, my voice thankfully even as I pushed by him and walked into the kitchen again.

I grabbed my notebook from the table, my bottom lip trembling and my eyesight blurry as I groped for the pen I knew was supposed to be right beside it. A small sob left me, and I dropped my notebook, slapping my hands over my mouth and closing my eyes tightly as I turned my back on the entrance of the room.

"Arianna?"

He was in there with me again, and I composed myself, sucking in deep breaths and digging my fingers into my eyes.

"Can I ask you something?" I asked, keeping my back to him.

"Yeah. Fine. Whatever."

"Why do you hate me so much?" I asked as casually as I could manage, pressing both hands over my heart, prepared to do my best to keep it intact for as long as I could.

"I don't hate you—"

"What did I ever do to you?" I continued, shrugging off his lie. "I've never said one bad word about you to anyone, never made fun of you when we were little and at our worst. I've never done anything to deserve the way you treat me, and I don't understand."

"It's not about you—"

"Yeah right, it isn't about me," I said, disbelief coloring my tone before I turned to face him. "I'm a waste of space, or I'd crush you if I sat on you, right? Isn't that what you and Steve said? Just because I'm heavier and I keep to myself, you all have the right to say these things to me?"

"It's just . . ."

"Just what, Evan?" I asked. "I'm just not good enough for you or your friends, right? So you're perfectly justified in saying those things to me because you don't think I'm good enough to talk to anymore. I tried to *help you.*" I swallowed hard and ran my hands through my hair. "I tried to be the better person because I could see that you were having a bad day, and all I wanted to do was help you out. Instead, you grab my wrist, bruise me, and insult me. How do you justify that?"

I turned to the side, wiping away the tears that had traveled down my cheeks during my rant.

"You can go," I said when he failed to say anything. "I'll talk to Mr. Streeter tomorrow and see if we can switch partners for this."

"No," he said. "We've already started—"

"Yeah, we got really far, didn't we?" I said sarcastically, crossing my arms over my chest. "I'm sure it won't be a big deal."

"No," he said again, his voice stronger. "Everyone else has already started, and no one will want to switch at this point."

"To work with you? I'm sure any of them will switch in a heartbeat. Maybe you can even join someone else's project."

"And what will you do?"

"Does it matter?"

"Yes."

"Why?"

"You'd be doing all the work yourself, on top of the work we'd have to get done for class. That's not fair."

"Since when have you cared about what's fair to me?" I asked, my voice low, even, and monotone. "I am nothing to you, Evan, and you've made that perfectly clear."

"Arianna . . ."

"I don't want you here," I said, and I was surprised that he looked almost apologetic. "I may not be able to say anything when I'm at school, but this is my house, and I don't want you here anymore."

He grabbed his notebook and leaned over the chair to pull his bag onto it. Then he grabbed all of his things and slung his bag over his shoulder.

"I'll see you tomorrow," he said over his shoulder as he turned.

"Yeah."

He walked out, the door slamming behind him. I walked the same path and flipped the locks before going back into the kitchen and grabbing my things. Back in my room, I collapsed onto my bed and stared at the ceiling.

The worst part about all of this wasn't that I'd be going it alone. The worst part was that he didn't have an answer to any of my questions. Yes, I'd interrupted him a few times, but in the end, he could have said something instead of just walking out. He didn't have an excuse. He didn't have a reason.

It just was.

And I was the butt of the jokes. I got the short end of the stick simply because I was different from the rest of them.

I couldn't wait until graduation.

Chapter Three

I saw the white orchid hanging off the locker as I walked down the hallway the next morning, but it didn't register. Guys were always sticking flowers of sorts into their girlfriend's lockers just to be cute and make them screech annoyingly for the rest of the morning, so I didn't think anything of it.

It was, however, unusual to see it hanging from *my* locker.

My bag fell from my shoulder, and my mouth dropped open as I stared at it. There had to be a mistake. This couldn't be right. Someone must have got the lockers switched and accidentally put it on mine.

Or someone was playing a joke on me.

I looked around the hallway and found that everyone was staring at me as well. I reached up with shaky hands and pulled it down. I nearly jumped out of my skin when a white note card attached to the stem fell down against the back of my hand. I flipped it open, my eyes widening when I saw the handwriting.

> *You were right.*
> *You don't deserve any of it.*
> *Let me make it up to you.*

I stared down at his words, my hands shaking as I traced over the writing with my fingertips. Maybe it was still a joke. Maybe he had some kind of hidden camera somewhere in the hallway, waiting for my reaction

Fourteen

d his friends could laugh over it for years to come. Or maybe
... ... to do it and wanted to see how far I'd let it go.

I grabbed my book bag and opened my locker. I shoved my book bag inside and grabbed my books, setting the flower carefully on top of my bag and untangling the note from it. I ignored everyone, kept my chin up, and I walked to class. I slipped inside, thankful that it was still empty, and walked over to my stool, plopping down onto it and resting my elbows on the table. Then I surreptitiously grabbed the note card from the top and flipped it open again.

It was his handwriting. I'd only gotten a few glimpses of it when I had attempted to help him pick up his papers, but it was unmistakable.

What was he doing? What was he trying to pull? This wasn't making any sense. This couldn't be right. Since when did anything I say to anyone actually have this kind of outcome?

I looked up when the door opened and my heart jumped into my throat as Evan walked in. I stared at him as he slowly walked over, then sat down in the empty stool beside me and carefully placed his books on the table.

"So?" he asked, looking over at me.

"What are you trying to pull?" I choked, looking down at the note again.

"I'm not trying to pull anything." I watched from the corner of my eye as he fidgeted with the edges of his textbook. "You've never done anything to me, and I never really gave you a chance. I'd like to . . ."—he sucked in a deep breath and sat up straight—"I'd like to get to know you."

"Who put you up to this?"

"Jesus Christ, Arianna, no one put me up to this." He sighed, exasperated. "This is something I want to do."

"Why?"

"Because you were right."

"I have a feeling I won't be hearing that phrase often."

"No, probably not."

I looked over at him and smirked when I saw the one on his face. I sighed and turned back to the note card.

"Fine. One chance, Evan. If you really want it, you've got it, but you won't get another one."

"I got it."

"Okay."

"Did you still want to switch partners?"

"I guess . . . not," I mumbled, hating myself and hoping that he meant what he was saying.

If he really meant everything he'd said, we'd get along just fine. The problem was I couldn't be entirely sure. In his opinion, he might've been taking a big chance on talking to me and befriending me, but it sure as hell felt like I was the one jumping off a cliff.

"There's a party at Steve's next weekend," he said slowly. "Would you like to go?"

I looked at him, wondering whom he thought he was talking to. Now, I was almost positive the flower had been a joke. He wanted *me* to go to a party full of people that would rather trip me than talk to me and treat me like a normal human being? He wanted *me* to go to a party that I wasn't even invited to with people that I couldn't stand.

"Are you serious?"

"Very."

"Why?"

"Are you going to stop asking me that question anytime soon?"

"Are you going to stop giving me cause to?"

He sighed, exasperated once again. "So that I can get to know you, and so that we can hang out a little."

"You want to get to know me at a crowded party with people that, as a rule of high school hierarchy, don't like me?"

"It's not like that."

"Really." I eyed him. "So everyone isn't going to look at me like they do when I'm here and say the exact same things they do while we're here, right? Things are going to magically change because we're not at school anymore?"

"I don't know. Maybe."

"You're not stupid, Evan," I said, my voice quiet. The door opened, and his head immediately snapped in that direction, and I clenched my jaw. "So stop thinking the best of your friends because different scenery won't change the things they say to me or how they treat me."

He looked at me, shifting uncomfortably and fidgeting as Brittany walked into the classroom.

"Hi, Ev!" Brittany squealed, prancing over to him and leaning against the edge of our lab table. "You know, I was thinking that maybe we should go out tonight."

She popped her gum, flipped her sleek blond hair over her shoulder, and giggled in a way that reminded me of an over-excited chipmunk. I rolled my eyes and shook my head, leaning an elbow on the table and resting my chin in my hand. I stared out the window, disappointed at how quickly I seemed to disappear from his radar.

He didn't want us to be seen talking, that much was obvious, but he wanted to get to know me somehow. This whole thing only solidified my thoughts about the orchid being a complete joke. I didn't understand why he would invite me to a party to "get to know me" but couldn't seem to bring himself to let the same people that were throwing the party see us talking at school.

I listened to Brittany and Evan flirt with each other, my heart sinking further in my chest when I realized that no matter how many times I told myself that I didn't like him anymore, I still did. I was as stupid as the rest of the girls in this high school, and there wasn't a damn thing that I could do about it.

I didn't notice when my other classmates started piling into the room, barely listened when Mr. Streeter called us to attention, and definitely didn't look at Evan the entire forty-five minutes that I had to be there. When the bell rang, I realized I had no idea what went on, and didn't know what we had to do for homework. I mechanically got up from my stool and gathered my books. Staring straight ahead, I walked out of the classroom and into the hallway.

At lunch I sat with Christina and Vince. I'd been sitting with them practically since kindergarten. They both had study hall first thing in the morning and had taken the option to have their parents write notes to get them out of it. We barely saw each other in the halls before lunch. They didn't know about the orchid—at least, they didn't mention anything to me if they did—and I wasn't ready to tell them the whole story just yet. I needed more time to work it out on my own before I brought my friends into it.

Plus, pretending that nothing was out of the ordinary almost made me forget that the opposite was true.

Dad was home when I got there, and I automatically made dinner for us. He wasn't a very good cook and while he did try his best, it usually ended up with the smoke detector going off. I had learned the basics of cooking from watching my mom do it, and when she was gone, I had taken over the responsibility of cooking.

We sat in silence as usual until I declared that I was done and went upstairs to start my homework. Around five thirty, the phone rang, and I ignored it until Dad called up the stairs that it was for me. I moved sluggishly down the stairs, offering him a small smile as I took the phone.

"Hello?"

"Um, hi, Arianna."

I didn't even have enough energy to slam the phone down, as I should have.

"Can I help you?"

"I, uh . . . are you all right? You just . . . you didn't seem like yourself after—" He stopped.

I stared hard at the floor. "How'd you get my number?" I finally asked.

"I know how to use a phone book. Are you all right?"

"Peachy."

"Did I do something?"

"Why would you think that?"

"You were just . . . you don't normally zone out like that is all. I just . . . Arianna, did I do something wrong?"

"Listen, Evan." I sighed. "Whatever you seem to want to pull off won't work if you're too embarrassed to be seen talking to me. I'm not a secret, and I refuse to be yours."

"You don't understand my friends, Arianna."

"Anna," I snapped.

"What?"

"I hate my full name, so stop it."

"Okay, well, *Anna*, you don't know what my friends are like. They need to . . . they need a warning."

"Should I wear a bright orange jump suit? Better yet, put me in a cage and smack a sign on the outside that says DON'T FEED THE ANNA. Hell, God knows I'd lose weight then, wouldn't I?"

"I've never said anything about—"

"You didn't have to. No one ever has to." I sighed and rubbed my forehead. "This is your choice, Evan. I was perfectly fine without talking to you." *The memories I have from when we were younger are better, anyway.* "You wanted another chance, and I gave it to you. You're not doing such a great job with it so far."

"I don't know how to act with you. You're not . . . you're not like the rest of them, and I don't know what the fuck I should do about it."

"Take me for what I am, Evan, or leave me alone."

"I can't exactly do that though, can I? We have a project—"

"That I told you I could easily get you out of," I said, interrupting him and running a hand through my hair. "This is your choice, and I'm not doing anything to influence you."

He was quiet, and I thought that he'd hung up before I heard a muffled curse. I closed my eyes and leaned back against the wall.

"I can't come over tonight," he finally said.

"I know. You have a date."

"Do you listen to *everything*?"

"When she's standing right there and has a voice like someone is slowly letting helium out of a balloon, it's kind of hard to miss, Evan."

He grunted, and I opened my eyes and slid down the wall, wrapping my arm around my upraised knees

"I have practice tomorrow night until five again, so I'll come over around quarter of. Is that okay?"

"That's fine."

"I'll talk to you tomorrow."

"Sure."

I could practically hear his teeth grinding, and I smiled to myself and played with the hem of my jeans.

"Bye, *Anna*."

"Bye."

I carefully set the phone down and stared at it for a few moments, tapping my fingertips against my thighs.

"Everything okay, Anna?" Dad yelled from the living room, his eyes no doubt focused on whatever documentary he was watching.

"Everything's fine, Dad." I sighed and stood up, starting back up the stairs. "Everything's just peachy."

~*~

I nearly screamed the next morning when I closed my locker door to find Evan standing behind it, his eyes darting nervously around the hallway while he shifted from one foot to the other. I raised my eyebrows and leaned against my locker as I stared at his profile and waited for him to actually look at me. After a few moments of him not looking in my direction, I obnoxiously cleared my throat and coughed to cover up the laugh when he jumped and almost dropped his books.

"I'm here. I'm talking. Hi. Good morning."

"Did someone slip something into your cereal this morning?" I asked casually.

"What? No. Why would you think that?"

"Because you're talking a mile a minute, and you're not really saying anything. If it bothers you that much, then go." I traced my tongue over my bottom teeth and stood up straight. "We both know that I'm not worth ruining your reputation."

"Why do you do that?"

"Do what?" I sighed, absently flipping my hair over my shoulder.

"Put yourself down like that."

"Like you don't do it."

He squared his shoulders and jutted out his chin. "I won't anymore."

I scoffed and rolled my eyes. "Until Brittany or Steve or Grace show up, right? Where the hell has Adam been, anyway? He hasn't been around to tell me I'm taking up the whole width of the hallway lately."

His face fell and his shoulders sagged. "He says that to you?"

"Yeah." I shrugged one shoulder and gripped the end of my long-sleeved shirt.

"He won't anymore," he said again.

"Right." I snorted. "I started on the paper last night. Did a lot of research and found a lot of things that could help." I looked up at him again. He didn't really seem very interested in that topic just yet, so I wracked my brain for something else to say. "How was your date?"

"It was fine, I guess."

"You guess?"

"She's just . . . a means to an end," he said, shifting uncomfortably in front of me.

"Ah."

"Yeah."

Awkward.

"Ev! Man! What the fuck are you doing over here?"

We both looked behind him to see Steve approaching, one of his eyebrows quirked up in amusement. He reached us and slapped a hand on Evan's shoulder, rolling his eyes at me before stepping in between us.

"I was just . . . uh, we were . . . ," Evan stuttered.

I rolled my eyes and sighed heavily, stepping out from behind Steve and clutching my books to my chest.

"We were just talking about our project," I said evenly.

"Right. Well, listen man . . . the party is going to be awesome!" he exclaimed, excited to the point where his voice rose an octave or two.

I started toward the classroom, mentally berating myself for thinking that he'd meant what he said.

"Anna!"

I stopped dead in the middle of the hallway and slowly turned on my heel to see Evan walking *away* from Steve and *toward* me.

It was as if time stood still. Everyone in the hallway stopped talking, stopped moving to turn and stare at Evan and then at me. I wanted to crawl into that hole I was waiting for and die because this could not truly be happening. He did not just walk away from Steve freaking Forrester to talk to me.

I was still gaping at him as he walked up to me with his head down and his eyes darting around the hallway.

"Are you feeling all right?" I asked.

"Funny."

"I'm being serious."

"This is what you wanted, isn't it?"

"No," I said. "It was your choice, Evan. I never said that I wanted anything from you."

"You are infuriating."

"I've never asked you for anything. You wanted another chance."

"And you seem to want the fucking world on a platter."

I opened and closed my mouth a few times, trying and failing to make sense of my jumbled thoughts.

"Yes, Evan, I have everything we need for our project. Thank you and I'll see you in class," I said loud enough for everyone to hear.

I turned on my heel again and started toward the classroom, pushing through the door and walking over to the empty lab table. I set my books down and rested my cheek on them, staring out the window and placing my arms on the table.

Evan didn't come in until everyone else had already been seated. He had Brittany wrapped around him, and I did my best to ignore everything as I meticulously opened my textbook to the assigned pages written on the chalkboard. As he sat down, I began reading the drivel on the page and doing my best to look engrossed in the monotonous world of—*hmm Polyatomic ions . . . Don't remember anything about that.*

"You're not making this very easy, you know," he said.

"This is who I am, Evan. Take it or leave it."

"You keep giving me that ultimatum. Do you want me to leave you alone?"

"I don't want to get hurt anymore." I looked at him and clenched my jaw. "And that's all you and your friends have done since middle school. I'm not sorry for making you work for something that I'm scared to give away to anyone." I sat up a little straighter, placing my hands in my lap. "Take it or leave it."

He stared at me until Mr. Streeter called us to attention, and I looked away. I had a lot to catch up on since I'd been so out of it yesterday, and I couldn't be concerned with Evan Drake staring holes into the side of my head.

I looked down when Evan slid a piece of paper underneath my hand, and glanced over at him. He tilted his head before looking back to the front of the room, and I sighed as I unfolded the paper and pulled it into my lap.

I'll take it and raise you a
secret that I guard with my life.
I have to wear a retainer to bed because
I sucked my thumb until I was thirteen.

My eyes widened, and I looked at him, crumpling the paper in my fist. He slowly looked back at me, the corner of his mouth twitching into a smirk.

"Seriously?" I mouthed, leaning forward.

He nervously licked his lips. I looked to the front of the room again. I kept the paper crumpled in my fist as I ripped out an entire sheet of paper from my notebook.

I won't tell anyone.

I folded it and slid it over to him, watching from the corner of my eye as he pulled it down into his lap and unfolded it. He grabbed his pen and awkwardly wrote on the note in his lap. He folded it back up and handed it to me underneath the table before looking up at the board and fidgeting with his pen.

Fourteen

You had to use an entire sheet
of paper for that? You're killing
trees that way, you know.

I rolled my eyes, placed the paper on the table, and grabbed my pen.

I just thought that you'd like to know.
And I didn't kill the damn tree.
Someone else killed the thing
and made paper out of it.
You're just as guilty!

I slid it over to him and stuffed it underneath his textbook. Resting my elbow on the table, I leaned my chin into my hand and forced myself to keep the smile off my face. I looked over at him when he slid the paper back over to me, and he openly grinned at me.

I use my notebooks for things
like schoolwork, Anna.
I do not use an entire sheet
of paper for a tiny little declaration.

Huffing, I stared at his handwriting and pursed my lips.

I'm sure you've never had letters
written to you, then, right?
Brittany hasn't tried to
compare you to a flower or anything?
Although, I'm not sure how
that would work seeing as how
she can barely pass gym class.

He laughed aloud as I slowly leaned away from him. Mr. Streeter fell silent, and I internally winced. Oh, this wouldn't be good.

"Is there something funny about this, Mr. Drake?" Mr. Streeter asked dryly, turning to look at Evan while holding a piece of chalk in his hand.

"Oh, well, you know . . . no?" he said, shrugging and laughing sheepishly. "I just . . . um . . . I was just thinking about something."

"Uh huh," the teacher said. "Think about human physiology, please."

"Right. Of course. Sure."

Mr. Streeter turned back to his chalkboard, and I relaxed a little and looked over at Evan. He was scribbling furiously, and I briefly wondered if that was a deal breaker. I took the folded paper from him, swallowing hard as I pulled it into my lap and unfolded it.

That was mean.
But completely true.

We ended our note with a confirmation that he was still coming over after practice, and I slipped the paper into the back of my notebook. Smiling to myself, I looked up at the board and listened to the rest of the lecture, feeling pretty good about what the rest of the day might bring.

~*~

I was late, getting back from my run and found Evan leaning against his car in the driveway. Looking down at my outfit, I groaned and stopped in front of him. I pulled my ear buds out and grabbed my iPod from my pocket.

"You run," he said.

"Yes." I turned off my iPod and wrapped the cord around it.

"I didn't know that." He pushed off his car.

"There's a lot you don't know about me, Evan," I said a little breathless as I wiped the sweat from my forehead with my sleeve.

"Like what?" he asked, following me as I walked up to the front door, pulling the key from my pocket and pushing it open wide enough so we could both get through.

"Like I'm a pretty damn good cook," I said and grabbed a bottle of iced tea from the refrigerator as I set my keys and iPod by the door.

"And?"

And? What more did he want to know? What did it matter to him?

"And I've been riding a dirt bike since I was old enough to ride a regular bike."

"You're kidding."

I smirked to myself and took a drink of my tea as I stared at the white door of the refrigerator. The one thing my father and I had always bonded over was dirt bikes and motocross. My mother had absolutely hated the whole idea, and whenever I mentioned wanting to compete, she quickly did her best to lay a guilt trip on me. It always worked.

I hadn't had the heart to do it since she'd died. It wasn't the same when my mother wasn't there to tell me how much she didn't want me to do it.

"No."

"Wow." I heard one of the chairs from the table scrape against the floor. "You were right, Anna. There is a lot I don't know about you."

I laughed. "Do you want something to drink?"

"Still have soda?"

I wordlessly opened the refrigerator, grabbed the green can, and walked over to him. I set it on the table in front of him, looked down at my clothes again, and finally realized what I was still wearing. I looked disgusting.

"I'm just going to uh . . . I'm going to change."

"You look fine, Ari . . . Anna," he said, correcting himself.

"I look like I just got back from running. I'll be right back. I have to get my stuff anyway."

"I found a few volunteers," he offered before I could take a step. "My parents and Sherri said that they'd be willing to help us out."

"Oh. Okay. I'll be right back."

I hadn't thought about why he was here, honestly. All that had been running through my mind was the fact that he was seeing me all sweaty, disgusting hair, and gross clothes; I didn't smell too great either.

I forgot that he was here so we could work on our project. I sucked in a deep breath and took the stairs two at a time, bursting into my room. I changed as fast as I could, spritzed some perfume on. I pulled my hair into a ponytail, hoping that it looked better than when it was down. I grabbed my book bag and walked back down the stairs. I walked into the kitchen and sat down in the chair across from him.

"Did you want to read what I wrote of the paper last night?" I asked as I pulled out my books.

"Yeah, sure. Let me know what you want me to look up, too, please? I meant it when I said I want to do half of it."

I was surprised that he was being so *nice* to me. I know that we'd seemed to have made some sort of non-verbal agreement to deal with this without ripping each other to pieces, but I was still shocked that he was keeping his word. I pulled my notes and the assignment out of my folder, sliding it across the table to him. He looked at the chair next to me and moved over, pushing his books with him and smiling awkwardly at me.

"It's just . . . easier."

"Yeah."

He read over what I'd written, and I flipped back to the page with my likes and dislikes from the other day.

I think you're beautiful.

I reached up and played with my ponytail, closing my eyes for a minute in an attempt to get rid of the memory. It wasn't something that I was fond of, and the less I thought about it, the better off I would be.

"Your perfume smells nice," he murmured, his eyes trained on the paper.

I looked at him, my mouth gaping open as my hand fell from my hair and slapped against the edge of the table. I winced, crying out a little when it landed on the bruises on my wrist, naturally. I pulled it against my chest, gently rubbing my fingers over it in an attempt to soothe it.

"Are you okay?"

"Yeah, fine."

He leaned forward, and I flinched back as he reached toward me.

"I'm not gonna hurt you," he said. He stared at my wrist and looked something very close to agonized. "I will never do that again."

I let him gently grab my fingertips and place my hand on the table between us. He carefully pushed back the sleeve of my shirt, and I blinked at him when he hissed.

"Shit, Arianna, I'm so fucking sorry," he whispered, actually sliding his hand underneath mine and wrapping his fingers around my palm. "I didn't . . . I was running so late, and I couldn't get anything into my locker like I should've and . . ." His eyes were still focused on my wrist. "You were right about everything. You were only trying to help and I—"

"Okay, listen," I said, my voice shaking as I slid my hand away and placed both of mine in my lap. "We'll start over, all right? We'll forget any of this happened, and we'll just start over."

"I can't just forget about this."

"Why not? It's not a big deal."

"It's a big damn deal, okay? A big fucking deal because I've never . . . I would never touch a girl that way. I've been raised better than that, and I just—"

"Because it was me," I said, looking down at the table. "And I'm supposed to be treated like shit by everyone."

"No. No, you're not. I had no right. None of us have any right." He leaned forward, buried his hands in his hair, and groaned. "We shouldn't treat *anyone* the way we've treated you, and it's not fair."

I sat, flicking my thumbnail against the bottom of the table.

"Let's just umm . . . we should really get started on the project," I said and grabbed the paper he'd dropped in front of him.

"Yeah, sure." He kept his head down and his hands in his hair for a few minutes longer. I fidgeted so I didn't feel so damned uncomfortable while he sat there, staring at the wood grains of my kitchen table.

After working for a few more hours, Dad finally arrived home and decided that he'd order pizza for dinner. I invited Evan to stay, but he declined, so we wrapped things up for the night.

Sighing, I stood up when Evan did. He slung his book bag over his shoulder. He kept his eyes down.

"I'll walk you out," I said. He turned on his heel.

I followed him out onto the porch.

"It's not fair, Anna," he whispered. "And I'm not going to do anything like that to you ever again. I'll make sure that no one else does, either."

I mentally scoffed before sighing and leaning against the side of the door.

"Evan, it's not a big deal."

"Yes, it is. No one deserves it. Least of all you." He stepped in front of me and placed his hand on my shoulder, squeezing gently, almost reassuringly. "I'll see you tomorrow morning."

I stared after him as he walked down the steps and got into his car. He waved at me as he pulled onto the street and drove away. I was completely flabbergasted. The Evan Drake that had just left my driveway didn't seem like the Evan Drake I'd gotten so used to seeing. He appeared to be caring and apologetic and completely unlike the guy he was in school.

I crossed my arms over my chest and smiled.

Maybe he did have some of that little boy I'd known all those years ago still inside of him.

"Anna? Are you going to just stand in front of the open door all night?" Dad called from the living room.

"Waiting for the pizza guy, Dad," I said absently, my eyes still glued to the same spot.

"Oh. Well. Okay then."

I rolled my eyes, closed the door behind me, and sat down on the first step. I rested my elbows on my knees and my chin in my hands while I wondered what in the hell tomorrow morning would actually be like.

Chapter Four

"Good morning, *Anna*."

I shrieked and nearly dropped everything as I leaned heavily against my car and rested my forehead on the roof.

"Sorry. I didn't mean to scare you."

I turned around when it felt like my legs no longer consisted of jelly and looked up at him.

It was wholly unnatural for someone to look that damn good in a casual outfit like jeans and a long-sleeved, red and blue striped shirt. It was wholly unnatural for someone that good-looking to be talking to me of his own free will.

"Good morning." He smiled and hooked his thumbs around the straps of his book bag. "Did you sleep well?"

I reached up, and he eyed my hand as much as he could before I placed it on his forehead. He shook my hand off, his eyebrow raised, as I shrugged and crossed my arms over my chest.

"Just making sure."

"I feel fine," he snapped.

"I was only joking around with you."

His nostrils flared for a moment, and he closed his eyes briefly.

"This isn't easy, you know."

"Yes, I'm very much aware of how easy it *isn't*, Evan." I rolled my eyes and walked by him, wondering how everyone in this school was a total moron. I made it through the front door of the school before I felt his hand in the crook of my elbow, pulling me into a random classroom.

Wow. He was quick. Then again, he was on the baseball team, so that kind of made sense.

He slammed the door behind us, and I shook myself free of him and looked down at my feet.

Here it comes, Anna. I hope you weren't really banking on having anything to do with Evan Drake for very long.

"I've never had to work for friends, Anna, because it never mattered to me before."

"Why does it matter now?"

"How the fuck should I know?"

I rolled my eyes.

"If this is too hard for you, no one's making you do anything with me or for me. I'm not a charity case, and I don't need someone like you, parading me around for I don't know what reason."

"You can't really be this dense!"

"I don't have time for this," I said and started to walk by him.

"You have just as much time as I do." He grabbed my arm again and stopped me. "Come on, just cut me a little slack, and meet me halfway here."

I looked up at him and found that his eyes were actually a very dark shade of blue. In the past, I'd only been close enough to see the basics—the slope of his nose, the curve of his mouth, the sharp angles of his jaw. I'd never gotten a chance to see the deep color of his eyes because he'd never been this close to me before, voluntarily.

The one time he was, I was too focused on the way he was crushing my wrist to register the color of his eyes.

"Sorry." I exhaled loudly, embarrassed to find that I was having a hard time doing much of anything.

"Don't apologize," he whispered, and I could've sworn he looked down at my lips before meeting my eyes again. That didn't make any sense. "Just . . . don't get so pissed off at me right away, all right? I'm really trying."

"Okay."

"We should uh . . . what do you say to hanging out later? Today, I mean. After school."

"Are we going to work on the project?"

"No. I mean . . . just hang out for a while. Get to . . ." He licked his lips, and my mouth went dry. "Get to know each other . . . without schoolwork and other people to worry about?"

I stared at him, doing my best not to look at his lips as he licked them again.

He *had* to stop doing that, or I was going to forget how to form complete sentences.

"Arianna?"

"Anna."

"Right. Anna." He shook his head sharply once. "What do you say?"

"To what?"

He gave me the most heartbreakingly beautiful smile, and I cleared my throat.

This is not good. Abort, Anna, abort!

"Yeah, sure, that's fine." I closed my eyes. "Where did you want to go?"

"Could we hang out at your place? My family is nosy, and bringing you home would only present questions neither of us really wants to answer."

My heart sank, and I nodded, taking a step back from him and opening my eyes to look down at my feet again.

Of course they would. They'd want to know why Evan—as close to high school royalty as anyone else in this place could get—was bringing home someone like me without the excuse of homework.

"Yeah, that's fine. I can meet you at the house, okay?"

"Yeah, okay. I'll be there right after you."

"We should . . . go to our lockers before the bell rings. Wouldn't wanna be late."

I attempted a laugh and looked up at him again. He was smiling at me, and I looked down at my feet again.

That smile was dangerous. He could've asked me to walk naked down the hallway, and I would've done it without a second thought.

This would've scared a number of people and possibly scarred them for life—including myself.

"No, wouldn't want that," he said.

I gave him a wry smile and started for the door, jumping back when he moved in front of me and pulled it open. I waited for him to walk ahead of me but looked up when he didn't move.

He was holding the door open for me.

Evan Drake was holding the door open for *me*.

I stammered my thanks and disappeared through the door. I kept my head down and my eyes glued to the floor as I walked to my locker. The hallway was completely silent, and I heard the door to the room Evan and I had just left slam shut.

I was quick to shove my things into my locker and grab the books I needed, all but running into the classroom and collapsing onto my stool. I crossed my arms over my books and buried my head in them, trying to calm all the crazy thoughts that were swirling around in my head.

~*~

I stared at Christina from across the table as her eyes followed Vince when he left the cafeteria. We had approximately five minutes before he came back, and she'd been staring holes in my forehead the entire time he sat next to her, rambling aimlessly about something no one cared to talk about.

In fact, *everyone* had been staring at me all day. I was surprised I didn't resemble a slice of swiss cheese at this point. I was more of a circus sideshow freak than I had been before, and I'd seriously begun to reconsider this whole let's-be-friends thing with Evan Drake thing. So far, it wasn't leading anywhere good.

"You spill and you do it *now*," Christina demanded, tapping fingernails on the grey surface of the cafeteria table. Her eyes danced with excitement as she wiggled.

"There's nothing to—"

"Don't start with that."

"He's my partner for human physiology, and we were just talking about the project."

"In an empty classroom? Alone? With the door closed and locked?"

"We wanted to talk in . . . hey." I sat up straight and pointed at her. "What are you talking about locked?"

"Don't think no one tried to get in, Anna."

"He didn't lock the door."

"Oh, so *he* locked it, huh?"

"It wasn't locked."

"Yes, it was. Brittany nearly had a freaking snit fit when she couldn't get in."

"Why would she think she needed to get in?" I grumbled, leaning forward, and resting my chin in my hand.

"Because she's Brittany Feldman," Christina retorted, grabbing the orange from Vince's tray and cradling it in her hand. "She's a pain in the ass and has to be shoved up Evan's for as long as possible each day."

I snorted. "She has a pretty good reason, though. I mean, he doesn't discourage her or anything."

"Seriously, tell me what's going on with you two," she said, leaning across the table and staring to peel the skin off the orange. "I won't tell anyone."

"No, I know," I said, fidgeting. "I just don't want to jinx anything especially if he changes his mind."

"Are you two dating?" she whispered.

"No," I exclaimed. "He'd never be interested in me that way. Christina, come on." I spared a glance up at her and rolled my eyes. "You know that's not the way things work."

"Things change, Anna. People change. If Evan got away from those idiots he calls friends, maybe you two would have a chance."

I shifted, biting down on the inside of my cheek to keep the hope swelling up inside my chest at bay. I didn't need to fuel the fire that shouldn't be there in the first place.

"Don't, Chris. Please."

She sighed as if I'd just asked her to go stand on the roof of the school and sing the latest Lady Gaga song. She leaned back as she pulled a piece of the orange apart and popped it into her mouth.

"We're trying to be friends. I think. I guess that's what we're doing?" I went back to fidgeting. "We're hanging out tonight."

"Where?"

"My house." I snorted halfheartedly. "He doesn't want to explain to his parents that we're just hanging out and not doing homework. I guess I'm not allowed to meet his family until I'm a size two."

Christina had her head tilted sympathetically to one side. Her jaw moved slowly as she chewed, and I sighed.

"People don't change, Chris," I said, trying to smile at her. "They just find new ways to work around their old personalities."

Vince chose that moment to sit down, reclaiming his spot next to Christina and wrapping his arm around her waist, pulling her against him and grinning at the both of us.

"Am I interrupting something?"

"Yes," Christina blurted out

"No." I laughed when Vince stared openly at Christina in disbelief. "We're done."

"You'd better give me details tomorrow," she said, leaning against Vince's shoulder and pointing at me.

"Yeah. Sure." I wished that Christina was right and maybe Evan could change after being a jerk for so long.

Too bad I wasn't dumb enough to actually believe that something like that could really happen.

~*~

I bolted from my car, barely closing the door behind me before jumping up the stairs and unlocking the door. I threw my keys on the table, chucked my book bag at the foot of the stairs, and looked around the room to make sure that it was clean.

It had been ages since I'd had anyone over after school. Christina and Vince would occasionally come over to hang out when we were at a loss for anything else to do around town, but they were the only ones. I didn't know what to do with someone new.

I walked into the living room and sat down on the couch, reaching for the remote on the coffee table and flicking on the television. I leaned back and changed the channel from the perpetual documentary programs.

I'd be lying if I didn't say I felt awkward. Sure, Evan had been over here to work on our project but never for anything else.

What was I doing? This would never work. This wouldn't get us anywhere. Now that he'd decided to stop abusing me and treat me like a person, all we'd done is make smart-ass comments to each other, and that was it. We couldn't build any sort of relationship on that. Friendship needed trust, and I most certainly did *not* trust him.

I groaned and threw the remote back onto the coffee table and rubbed my hands over my face.

This was insane. It wouldn't prove anything. I was sure he was very much aware of that, and would have a grand ol' time telling all of his little minions everything he thought he'd be able to get from me.

He probably didn't even have a retainer. His teeth were gorgeous. Straightest teeth I think I'd ever seen. If the college thing didn't work out for him—assuming he was going to college—he could star in one of those toothpaste commercials.

"Anna Weller, you are an idiot," I declared and stood up.

I almost jumped through the roof when I heard a knock on the door and sat back down, my pulse racing. There was another knock and I stood up, slowly making my way to the door. Exhaling heavily, I turned the doorknob and yanked back on it. Evan stood in the doorway, shifting his weight and tapping his hands against his thighs.

"Hey," he said, chuckling nervously.

"Hey."

I moved out of the way, and he walked in, looking around the hallway as if he hadn't already seen it plenty of times.

"So . . ." I stepped back to his side and pushed my hair behind my ear. "What did you . . . what'd you wanna do?"

"Well . . . I hadn't really thought of that. I guess . . . we could talk, right?" He crossed his arms over his chest and looked down at me.

"Yeah, sure." I motioned to the living room and waited as he walked ahead of me and plopped down into the spot on the couch I'd just been sitting in. I sat on the other end and turned to him. "How was the rest of your day?"

"It was school, you know? Sucked. Yours?"

"Sucked, too," I said.

"Did anyone . . . you know, say anything to you? About me?"

"Just Christina." I looked down at my lap. "Everyone else just gave me dirty looks."

"Sorry."

I looked up at him again, shrugging before looking down to my lap.

"It's not your fault."

"I was the one that dragged you into an empty classroom."

"Why'd you lock the door?" I asked, looking up at him once again.

"It kept the conversation strictly between us, didn't it?"

"Well, yeah, but everyone else is thinking that we . . . I don't know what they're thinking, but it wasn't that we were just having an innocent conversation about our project."

"Is that you what you told Christina?"

"No. I told her that we were going to hang out tonight." He winced. "You don't want anyone else to know."

"Anna . . ."

"I knew this wasn't going to work." I pulled my legs up onto the couch. "Christina isn't going to say anything."

"It's not that I didn't want anyone else to know. I just don't know how they're going to take it."

"Is it at all possible for you to think for yourself?" I asked, looking at him. "Forget about the idiots who cling to your every word for one second? Did you ever think that maybe I'm a pretty awesome person? That we'd get along well if you could just stop for one second to realize it?"

"They're my friends, Arianna," he said through his teeth.

"They're idiots, Evan," I shot back.

"You're doing the same thing to them that you're accusing me of. You're aware of that, aren't you?"

I stared at him and snapped my mouth shut.

"At least I have a legitimate reason to not like them," I said. "There is no reason whatsoever that they couldn't talk to me or get to know me."

"Like I'm doing right now."

"Why?"

"Why do you always have to—" He rubbed his forehead before glaring at me. "I feel guilty, Arianna."

"Then get out," I said, looking away from him and staring at the bottom of the television stand.

I should've been used to getting hurt by now, but every time he opened his mouth and said something like *that*, it just got ten times worse.

"You can't just send me away every time I say something that you don't want to hear!"

"You haven't stopped to listen to *anything* I might've said to you in the past so why in hell should I listen to you?" I snapped.

"Because I'm here!" he shouted. "I'm here, trying to make it right with you! You have to give me some room to breathe!"

"Why should I?"

"Because we can't make this work if you don't give too! I know that you're pissed and you have every right to be, but dammit, Arianna, I can't do this completely on my own."

I blew out a deep breath and closed my eyes, resting my chin on my knees and doing my best to clear my head.

"Anna . . ."

"Give me a minute," I said, holding up my hand.

I could see his point. I wasn't making it easy for him, and while he didn't deserve easy, it wasn't fair that I kept making him jump through hoops if I wasn't really going to make an effort. I had years of anger stored up for him and his friends, but at least he finally had found the guts to make an effort with me.

"You need to understand that I don't understand anything," I said after a few moments of silence. "I don't understand why I'm always the target, and I don't understand why you're trying to get to know me now." I sucked in a deep breath. "No, wait. You feel guilty. Right."

"I do," he said, and I felt my heart shrink back just that much further in my chest. "But I wasn't lying when I said that you were right and that you didn't deserve anything we'd ever done to you. I do want to know you, Arianna."

"Then you need to stop using my full name because I *will* hurt you."

I opened my eyes and looked to find that he was staring at the palms of his hands.

"Steve is an asshole," he said "There's no excuse for him and what he said about you sitting—"

"I get it," I interrupted and wrapped my arms tightly around my legs.

"You're not that big, Anna."

I scoffed and rolled my eyes, tightening my hold on my legs and staring at the remote on the coffee table.

"You seemed to agree with him a few days ago."

"You ran out of the classroom before you could hear me tell him that he was being an ass."

I slowly looked at him to find that he was still staring at his palms.

"What?"

"That was uncalled for." He turned his hands over only to stare at the backs of them instead. "He wanted to get a rise out of you, and he got it." He looked at me, staring directly into my eyes. "I told him that he was being an ass."

"Why didn't you say anything when he asked about me . . . molesting you?"

I nearly choked on the word.

"I was being an asshole too." He conceded turning his hands back over and flexing his fingers.

"Why did you say that you thought I was beautiful as your lie?" I asked, chewing on the inside of my cheek.

"I copped his attitude for the rest of the day, and everyone else teased me about defending you. I was pissed, and I took it out on you because at the time, you were the one that caused all of it for me. I took a lot out on you, and I shouldn't have."

"I don't want to be your scapegoat anymore."

"And I'm going to try really hard to make sure that you aren't."

"Okay." I went back to staring at the coffee table, still chewing on the inside of my cheek as I felt him shift around on the other end of the couch.

"Hey, can we start over?" he asked after a few silent moments.

I shrugged and picked at the hem of my worn-out jeans. "Yeah, whatever."

I stared at him with my mouth open when he stood up and headed for the door. I rolled my eyes at his back and rested my chin on my upraised knee when he walked out. I guess his version of starting over and mine were very different. At least my version kept him in the same room.

"Jerk," I said under my breath.

Once again, I heard a knock at the door. Snapping my teeth together, I unfolded myself from the couch and pulled open the door to find Evan standing on the other side.

"Anna!" he exclaimed with a smile on his face.

I blinked at him. He seriously walked outside and knocked on my door *again*.

"You are some kind of crazy." I laughed.

He shrugged innocently, and I moved out of the way, letting him back into the house. I stared at the back of his head, not sure what I was supposed to do now that we were in the same position we'd been in a few minutes ago.

"Do you want something to drink?" I asked finally, tapping the balls of my hand against my thighs.

"Mountain Dew?"

I went to the fridge, grabbed the can and a bottle of tea for me. When I returned to the hallway, he was nowhere to be found, so I peeked around the stairs. He was sitting back on the couch and staring at the television. I shuffled over to him and handed him the can before taking my place back on the couch and twisting the top off my tea.

"What's your favorite show?" he asked, turning to look at me as he popped the top of the can.

"*Grey's Anatomy*, I guess."

"What's the obsession everyone has with doctor shows?" he asked, his face serious as he turned to me and cupped the can in his hands. "They're all the same."

"In a sense," I agreed, and turned to him. "The storylines are different, though. So are the personal lives of the characters."

"How many times can you watch a doctor go in for surgery, though, honestly? My mother loves that show too, and I just don't understand the appeal."

I laughed and shrugged, sipping from my bottle.

"The actors are pretty."

"Oh!" He chuckled. "Pretty actors make all the difference."

"Usually."

"I see."

"What's yours?"

"*Ghost Hunters.*"

I raised an eyebrow at him, and he fidgeted, tapping against the sides of the can.

"Really?"

"It's the only show I watch. Sherri has this thing with ghosts and all that." He shrugged again. "It's interesting."

"My dad and I used to watch that all the time," I said. "Now it's all documentaries and history and poker."

"Your father watches poker?"

I chuckled. "Sometimes he'll get together with some of his buddies and have a poker night."

"Here?"

"Oh, no." I scoffed, waving at him. "He always goes to their place."

"You and your dad don't seem close." I looked up at him and shrugged, picking at the green label on my bottle. "I figured that you would be. Since it's just the two of you . . ." His voice trailed off.

"You figure things a lot for not knowing me that well."

"Sorry." He looked down and brought the can up to his mouth.

We sat in silence once again as he played with the top of his can, and I stared down at my lap in an attempt to think of something to talk about.

"You said that you cooked, right?"

"Yeah."

"Can you make homemade macaroni and cheese?"

"Of course."

"Will you show me?" he asked.

"You seriously want me to teach you how to make mac and cheese?"
He shifted uneasily.

"It's my favorite and the only version I ever liked was my grandmother's. She passed away three years ago, and my mom just can't . . ." He took another sip. "She tries."

"All right," I said, standing up. "I'll show you how to make it."

He grinned—nearly stealing my breath—before he popped up. The way his face lit up and even the way his eyes seemed to brighten and widen a little, made him look like a kid on Christmas morning.

"You really have to wear a retainer?" I asked, tilting my head to the side as I looked at his teeth.

They were all pearly white, straight, and perfect.

"Yes, I really do. Makes me drool. Not a pretty picture."

I laughed and rolled my eyes, as I turned on my heel and started toward the kitchen.

"Attractive, Drake."

"Yeah, well, it's the truth."

I laughed and set my tea on the table as I pulled out two saucepans and placed them on the stove.

"Are you ready?"

He nodded enthusiastically and set his can on the table as well, rocking back and forth on his heels.

"Well, get over here," I said, waving him over as I sidestepped toward the refrigerator. "There's a bit to do."

He was by my side almost as soon as I said it, his hands behind his back as he watched me gather everything from the fridge and place the items on the counter.

I still wasn't entirely sure what to do with him. He seemed like he meant everything he'd said. And why would he tell me something like having to wear a retainer to bed or watching a show like *Ghost Hunters*—two things that would definitely hurt his popularity—if he hadn't meant anything he'd said? I didn't trust him, and I probably wouldn't for a long time, but at least this was a step in the right direction.

It had to be the right direction. I couldn't handle the wrong one.

Chapter Five

There was something distinctly different when I walked into the school the next morning. Granted, it was Friday, and it always felt that way because it was just before the weekend. People were either making plans or fine-tuning the ones they already had, and there was a certain energy about the entire student body.

I was just happy for the two days I wouldn't have to see these people, two days I'd have the house mostly to myself while dad went golfing with his buddies, and two days to relax and just be me.

I was in a good mood, though. I'd had a good time hanging out with Evan last night, and the high hadn't worn off quite yet. I was still wary of him and at certain points during the night, it had been extremely awkward between us. We'd done homework while the macaroni and cheese cooked, and he'd told me that he'd asked a few of his friends to volunteer for him. We both agreed that he could do that on his own. Dad came home around six thirty again. He inhaled and hummed appreciatively before disappearing into the living room. While the night hadn't started out that great, overall it hadn't ended horribly, either.

Today, however, it felt like I was walking to my doom as I stepped into the hallway and made my way to my locker. Every single person turned to look at me as I walked, and I played with a piece of my hair and kept my head down. My heart beat hard against my ribs.

What really sealed the deal, though, was when Kyle, Evan's best friend, stopped me in the middle of the hallway in front of everyone with his girlfriend Ashley James by his side. He looked as uncomfortable and nervous as I felt. He resembled a short pit bull with spiky blond hair, and his eyes were a beautiful deep green. Kyle's nose had been broken a few times, the bumps prominent and something he was very proud of. Still, he was attractive, and sometimes he snorted when he laughed. His front teeth were crooked, presumably for the same reason that his nose had been broken so many times—sports. He was on the football team and the baseball team, and while I didn't go to many games, I knew from all the other students and posters that he played hard. His loud, deep voice was hard to miss, and while he was nice to everyone he came into contact with, he mostly stayed in the same circle that Evan did.

Kyle and Ashley had been on-again, off-again until the beginning of the school year.   Now they were one of the power couples. She was beautiful—with her shoulder-length, brown hair, perky upturned nose, heart-shaped lips, and a petite but powerful body toned from years of gymnastics. She had her core group of friends, didn't venture outside of her social circle, and had her digital camera practically glued to her hand. A moment ago, I was sure she didn't know I existed.

Ashley never looked uncomfortable or nervous. Neither did Kyle for that matter, and neither of them had *ever* acknowledged me in front of everyone.

"Anna, could we talk to you for a minute?" he asked, slinging an arm around my shoulders and steering me in the opposite direction.

I thought I heard an audible gasp from everyone.

"I have to put my books away, Kyle," I said, trying to wiggle out from underneath his arm.

"You can put your stuff in my locker for now."

"Why?"

"Because I want you to walk with us."

I thought that either he'd lost his mind completely or there was another one of those invisible memos about me not being a diseased outcast for the day.

"To where?"

"Uh . . . to . . . ."

"The gym!" Ashley exclaimed, grabbing Kyle's other arm and pulling us both in the direction of the gymnasium.

"For what?" I asked.

"I feel like we don't talk enough, Anna, and I want to remedy that."

"Kyle, seriously, what's going on?"

I dug my heels into the floor and almost tripped over my own feet when Kyle kept walking. I slipped out from underneath his arm as they both turned to look at me.

"Nothing's going on, Anna." Ashley laughed nervously.

For all the confidence she seemed to ooze, I never thought she knew how to laugh nervously. It was strange and made the horrible feeling I had even worse.

"Then why did you drag me away like that?"

"Uh, well . . . I just thought . . . I told you. We should talk more," Kyle stammered.

"Let's do it later, then. I need to put my books away."

I walked around both of them.

I could still feel the stares, and I heard footsteps behind me. I looked over my shoulder and saw Kyle and Ashley trailing behind me, both of them looking dejected and still really nervous and uptight. Whispers were bouncing off the walls of the eerily quiet hallway as I walked, and I ran a trembling hand through my hair.

I stopped in front of my locker and gasped. *Cow* was written in black marker across the top. *Heifer* was written vertically underneath it. *Pig* was written next to *heifer*. And in the middle was a computer-generated picture of a cow's body with my head attached to it. I placed one hand on my throat, gently dragging my fingernails down as if that would help me breathe.

"Anna," I heard Kyle say from behind me.

I held up a hand, my eyes still glued to the scene in front of me.

I should have seen this coming. It was the next logical step. It actually wasn't as bad as some of the stuff they could have done, but it was still a shock to see it written so boldly.

I ran my hand down the front of my blue sweater and did the same with my other. I pulled on the bottom of my shirt, trying to make it longer somehow, even though it already hit mid-thigh. Anything that would hide the small roll that showed through the fabric. In all honestly, I wanted to pull the shirt over my head entirely, but pulling it over my head would leave me vulnerable to unseen attacks. I'd be exposing more of my body, and they would be able to see it.

Ashley placed her hand on my arm. "Anna."

I flinched away from her, briefly wondering if she was in on it. She was one of *them*; she could've known all about it. Kyle too. Maybe they were both in on it; maybe the person who had done it had just finished, and they needed to buy a little time.

I didn't know what to do. I felt as though I couldn't do anything but stand there and stare at it. It didn't seem real. Why would someone do this? Why did they do any of the things they'd ever done to me in the past?

"Because you're a cow," I whispered, answering myself.

"Anna, don't believe—" Kyle said.

"Don't," I whispered and turned around. "Just . . . don't."

I walked between Kyle and Ashley with my head down. The blood rushed in my ears and tears filled my eyes as I walked down the hallway, roughly shoving through the double doors and back into the parking lot.

I didn't care if I missed school. I didn't care about anything except for getting out of there. I couldn't stand to be in that place for one more minute, and the last thing I wanted to do was go through an entire day with *them*.

"Anna?"

I heard his voice but kept walking, my head still down as I stared hard at the pavement. I didn't want to be around anyone right now or risk damaging any progress Evan and I might have made last night. If there were even a small fraction of a chance that Evan and I could be friends, then this would definitely not be the time to talk to him.

I was quick to get back into my car and shove the keys into the ignition. Staring straight ahead, I pulled out of my space and drove toward out of the parking lot, blinking and sniffling the entire way. After making it home in record time, I jumped out of the car, dashed into the house and up the stairs, collapsed onto my bed, and buried my face in my pillow.

The tears started, the sobs came, and I wrapped my arms around myself in a sad attempt to keep myself together.

~*~

I shouldn't have walked out. I should've stayed and dealt with it. Running away didn't prove anything and probably only made them all happy that they'd gotten to me.

I didn't understand what I'd done this time. The only thing I'd done differently was talk to Evan, and that was mostly because I had to. He'd done the rest and had seemed to truly want a chance to get to know me. Why had I been cut down for what he'd wanted in the first place?

I sniffled and wiped my cheeks, staring at the wall of my bedroom and curling into the fetal position on my bed.

I didn't know what time it was. I didn't know how long I'd been up in my room. School could've been over for hours now, and I wouldn't have known the difference. Hell, it could've been early Saturday morning, and I wouldn't have realized. The dark sky outside my window told me it was nighttime.

I sighed heavily when I heard footsteps outside my bedroom door and sucked in a shaky breath, once again wiping off the tears from my cheeks with the sleeve of my shirt. There was a knock on the door but I didn't move, figuring my dad had gotten home and wanted to know why I hadn't bothered to come down or fix dinner for us.

I squeezed my eyes shut, pretending to be asleep and hoping that he would just go away when I heard the door open. A few seconds later, I heard it close again, and I sighed, pushing my hair out of my eyes.

"Anna?"

I jumped as I heard a voice that clearly did not belong to my dad and turned to face the door. His profile was visible from the streetlights outside my window, and I tensed.

"What?" I managed to say, my voice rough and my throat raw. "How'd you get in here?"

"Your father let me in."

Huh. He *was* home. Glad he came up to see if I was all right.

"What do you want?" I curled up even tighter under my comforter and stared blankly ahead.

"I wanted to see if you were all right."

I looked up when I heard the floorboards creaking underneath his weight as he walked over to me. I kept my eyes on his dark figure as he lowered himself to the floor, resting his arms on the edge of my bed and placing his chin on his hands.

"I'm fine."

"It shows," he said.

I stared at him, his face partially hidden in shadows.

"I would've been here earlier," he said after a few moments of silence, "but coach kept us later for practice because it was a Friday."

"Did you have anything to do with it?"

"No!" he exclaimed. "No . . . ," he repeated, quieter.

We once again sat in silence. "Who was it, Evan?" I whispered.

He sighed heavily and tilted his head to the side. I huffed, closing my eyes as he reached out to rub his thumb over my cheek.

"Brittany and Grace," he whispered back.

"Why?"

"Because of me." He pushed his hand back and into my hair, his thumb still stroking my cheek. "I'm sorry, Anna."

I closed my eyes when I felt them water again and turned to bury my face back into my pillow. He slid his hand to the back of my head, his fingers still tangled in my hair, and I did my best to keep my emotions under control.

It was bad enough that he'd caught me in my room, sitting in the dark and moaning over my bad day. It would be even worse if he saw me cry.

He kept his hand in my hair, gently scratching the back of my head as I did my best to either smother myself or calm myself down. I hadn't quite figured out which I wanted to do more.

"What do you say to dinner or something?" he asked after a while.

I turned my head and his hand fell out of my hair and away from me. I looked over at him through blurry eyes.

"Is this guilt?" I asked, my voice shaking.

"Part of it," he said. "I said I wouldn't let this happen, and it did."

"What's the other part?"

"The other part is that my new friend needs a friend and I'm . . ." He exhaled, placed his hand on my back. "I'm here for you."

"This isn't just another way to humiliate me somehow?"

"No."

I stared at him, and he caressed my back.

"I'm not really hungry."

"How about we go see a movie then?"

"It's a Friday night. Don't you have plans?"

"I did, but I don't anymore."

"With Brittany?"

"Yeah."

"Evan—"

"A few days ago I wouldn't have thought anything about this," he admitted, still scratching my back. "I probably would've laughed, said you deserved it, and never would've given it another thought."

I gasped and buried my face back into my pillow.

"A few days ago, I wouldn't have thought about how this would have made you feel because it didn't matter to me. A few days ago, I didn't *know* you."

"You don't know me now," I said.

"I'm trying to. And I was hoping that you were trying to know me, too."

Looking over at him, I flicked on the lamp on my bedside table, hissing when the sudden invasion of light hit my eyes. He grunted and rubbed his eyes as I propped myself up on my elbows and stared at my headboard.

"Can I ask you a question?" I glanced at him.

"Yeah."

"You . . . hated me a few days ago. How did that change so quickly?"

"I never really hated you, Anna. I just didn't think about anyone's life but my own. I never gave much thought to anyone that wasn't in my circle, and I didn't think about what happened once everyone went home for the day. It's like I . . . I separated it, I guess. My home life is different from my school life, and I just thought that everyone else did the same thing."

He stared at me with something very close to a pout on his face.

"Words are powerful weapons, Evan."

He looked away and reached up again, sliding his hand underneath my pillow. He grabbed my hand, pulling it out into the light and turning my wrist to look at the yellowish bruises that were still on my skin.

"I know that now." He shifted, rising up and gently covering my wrist with his other hand. "I'm trying to make it right."

"I'm really trying to believe you." I looked down at our hands. "But it's going to take more than a few days for me to trust you when I've got years of hurt piled up."

"I know that," he said. "I'm just asking for that chance, Anna. You said that I had it."

"You do."

"So come out with me tonight. We can go see a movie, and if you're hungry after that, we'll go out to dinner. It's a start, right? We need a start."

I stared down at him. He squeezed my hand, stood up, and then helped me off my bed. Then, without warning, he wrapped me in his arms and buried his nose in my neck. I stood stiffly against him, staring over his shoulder at my wall in shock.

"I really don't deserve it. Thank you."

"S-sure." I stepped away from him.

"Will your father mind?"

"I didn't even know that he was home before you told me he let you in."

"I'll take that as a no."

I pulled on the hem of my sweater, nervously looking around my bedroom, and for the first time, I realized that Evan Drake was *in my bedroom*. The clutter and the drawings I'd had taped to the walls since I was little were out in the open, and he could now finally see it all.

Looking at it now, I really needed to redecorate. This room belonged to someone that was maybe entering high school, not getting ready to graduate and go off to college.

"I just need to use the bathroom," I said. "You can . . . uh, you can wait up here or downstairs if you want."

"I'll wait in the hallway."

I followed behind him as he walked out, detouring into the bathroom and closing the door behind me. Then I leaned against it and closed my eyes tightly.

I could do this.

~*~

My face fell as we pulled into the parking lot of the movie theater, and I heard Evan curse under his breath as he turned off the car.

"Did you plan this?" I asked, staring at Steve, Brittany, Grace and Adam as they stood at the entrance to the theater.

"What? No! I had no idea they'd be here, Anna."

I looked over and stared at him for a few moments. Deciding I could trust him, I looked out the windshield and said, "Can we go somewhere else?"

He chewed on his bottom lip thoughtfully, looking at his friends and then back at me.

"No. Come on."

"Evan, I don't want to deal with them."

"I have an idea."

"What is it?"

"Just get out of the car, okay? Trust me."

I stared at him in disbelief as he got out of the car. I threw my hands in the air and then pushed open the door and got out.

The day really couldn't get much worse at this point, so I might as well let him do whatever it was that he was so intent on doing.

He rounded the front of the car and stood in front of me, making sure to lock eyes with me as he reached out and grabbed my hand. I raised an eyebrow at him as he linked our fingers together and wondered if he could hear the stampede in my chest right where my heart was.

"What are you doing?" I asked, stretching out the words.

"We're going to see a movie," he said with a shrug.

"You're . . . we're . . . they'll think we're on a date."

"So then I guess we're on a date, aren't we?"

I gaped at him.

What?

"Run that by me one more time," I managed to say, circling my finger in the air and blinking at him.

"Then I guess we're on a date," he said.

"To them, right? That's just what we'll say to . . . to them, right?" I stuttered, looking away from him and over to the group.

Huh. I didn't know Grace smoked.

I closed my eyes, and placed my hand on my forehead. There were more important things going on right now, and I was wondering about Grace's smoking habits? Evan Drake was either taking me on a date or getting me all worked up just to humiliate me. Both of these scenarios made me nervous as hell, and after the day I'd had, right about now I wished I were back in my bed.

"Well . . . no."

I snapped my head in his direction and dropped my hand to my side.

"Are you serious right now?"

"Yeah." He looked down at his feet and tapped his toes against the pavement.

"You're not feeling right, are you?" I asked.

"I'm feeling just fine, Anna."

"This is insane. You've lost your mind."

"Or I found it."

"You're like Jekyll and Hyde!" I exclaimed.

"Keeping you on your toes, though, right?" He gently swayed our still joined hands and laughed nervously.

"Oh, I'm on something, all right. Am I awake? Am I even really awake?"

"Yes, you're awake." He stepped in front of me. "Give in a little, Anna, please," he whispered.

I closed my eyes and acquiesced.

He was trying, and now I needed to as well. Friendship—or whatever we were doing right now—was a two-person effort, and I needed to give in.

Opening my eyes, I said, "This isn't a joke to you."

"I'm being dead serious right now."

"You're really taking me out on a date."

"I'm really taking you out on a date," he said, grinning down at me.

Yes. My heart had officially stopped.

"Okay," I said with a shaky voice.

"Okay?"

"Okay."

"Okay." He grinned, backing away and pulling on my hand as he walked to the entrance of the theater. "Ignore them, all right?"

"Yeah, sure. Ignore them. Right."

"Hey." He stopped us before we'd taken more than three steps, and I swallowed hard. "Just relax."

"I don't know how," I admitted sheepishly. "Not around you, not around them. I just . . . I don't know how to."

He sighed, and I half expected him to call off the whole thing. I was very much ready to walk back to the car until he spoke.

"And that's my fault." I stared at him. "I'm so sorry, Anna."

I shrugged, looking away from him and over to the entrance. His friends were openly gaping.

"We've been spotted," I stage whispered.

He looked over his shoulder and then back at me, squeezing my hand.

"Ready to start our date?"

"It's gonna take a minute to get used to that."

He laughed, once again leading me toward the entrance. I squared my shoulders as we approached them, my heart beating rapidly, and I wondered briefly if all this activity was going to give me a heart attack. I did my best to ignore the group.

"You ditched me for *her*?" Brittany sneered.

"Yeah," Evan said simply. "I did."

"Are you going blind, dude?" Adam asked, stealing the cigarette from

Fourteen

Grace.

"Nope. In fact, I'm pretty sure my eyes are wide open."

"This has gotta be some kind of charity thing, right?" Steve asked, stepping in front of Evan. "Dude, we've never gone down this road. There are plenty of other girls—"

"Yes, there are. I wanted to be with Anna tonight." He shrugged, and I did my best to ignore them. Easier said than done, but at least Evan wasn't agreeing with them this time. "See you all Monday morning."

"I'm calling you tomorrow. I wanna know what the fuck you're on tonight," Steve taunted, tapping Evan's shoulder before moving out of the way.

"My answers won't change, Steve."

"You have," Grace scoffed.

"Maybe so," he said, and we started toward the doors again as he yelled over his shoulder, "Maybe I don't wanna be an asshole anymore."

With that, he pulled me into the theater after him, and we stood in line for tickets. I didn't know what to say, so I kept my eyes focused on the brightly lit board with all the movies listed. He was still gripping my hand, and I jerked when he flexed his fingers. I let go of his hand and took a step to the side.

"Hey," he said, reaching out for me again. "You were just crushing my hand there."

"I was?"

He took a step toward me again, sliding his arm around my shoulders and pulling me back to him. I leaned against him, not having any idea what to do with my hands or how to act or what I was even supposed to say. He made me so nervous that not all the dating rules I'd learned in the past, applied here.

Now I was in an alternate universe because that would make more sense than this crazy night I was having. Nothing like this had ever happened to me. Guys like Evan Drake did not hold my hand or put their arm around me, and they definitely didn't take me out on dates.

"You're stronger than you appear to be," he continued, moving up when the line did.

"Have to be. Sorry."

"Me too. What do you want to see?"

"Comedy," I said. "Definitely comedy."

"You read my mind. Comedy it is."

He paid for my ticket, *he* bought me a box of snowcaps and a drink, *he* was the one to hold my hand all night, and *he* was the one that kept an arm around my shoulders as we walked out when the movie was over.

"Are you hungry yet?" he asked as we walked outside.

As I looked at his hand dangling off my shoulder, I summoned up all my courage and laced our fingers together, my heart fluttering when he immediately squeezed my hand. I looked up at him, surprised, and he just smiled back.

"I could eat."

"All right then. What would you like? Denny's or Friendly's?"

"Going for the big time, huh?"

He laughed, and my breath caught when he leaned in and bumped his nose against my temple.

"Two of my favorite restaurants," he informed me. "If there's someplace else you'd like to go, I'm more than happy to take you there."

"No," I said, choking on my words. "Denny's is fine."

"All right then." We made it to the car, and he opened the door for me, grinning brightly when I raised an eyebrow at him. "This is still a date, Anna."

"You take all your dates to Denny's?"

"No." He chuckled. "You're just special-er than the rest of them."

I laughed and smacked his arm.

"Mm-hm. Sure."

"I mean it! Half the time, we don't make it to the restaurant."

"So you just leave them there after the movie?"

"No. We get a bit distracted."

"Distracted?"

He shifted uncomfortably.

"With . . . lips and—"

I held up my hand to stop him. "Got it. No more explanation is needed." I looked down at the front seat of the car before eyeing him questionably. "Maybe a little more explanation is needed."

"It was always the backseat." He chuckled nervously.

"Well, as long as the front seat is safe."

"Totally safe. I promise."

"Okay then."

I finally slid into the seat and placed my hands on my knees, looking up at him as he continued to stand there and look down at me.

Fourteen

"You take things like that so . . . easily."

I leaned forward, splaying my hands out on my knees and shrugging.

"Should I freak out or something?"

"Most girls that I've taken on dates would've."

"Well, I'm not most girls," I said. "You're going to have to get used to that."

He licked his lips and crouched down, balancing on the balls of his feet. "I want to take you out again."

"Really?"

"Really. Are you okay with that?"

"Uh . . ." I looked down at my lap and pressed my lips together. "Yeah, I guess so."

"Are you sure? I'm not going to do a single thing to make you uncomfortable ever again, Anna."

"I'm sure." I barely hid my smile. "Thank-you."

"All right." He stood. "Denny's, here we come."

I laughed as he closed the door and leaned back in the seat, running my hands through my hair.

I can do this. I can do this. I can do this. I can do this. I will do this. Hell, I am doing this.

~*~

"So . . . ," Evan said as he parked in front of my house and placed his hands in his lap, "I have plans with my family tomorrow but, uh, if you want to, you know, hang out later? I could . . . I'd like that."

I blinked at him. He sounded nervous.

We'd spent the entire dinner learning new things about each other; he liked sci-fi novels and old black and white movies. Soft jazz relaxed him, which surprised me beyond words because it was my favorite type of music to listen to when I needed time to sort through everything in my life; and while he enjoyed going to parties sometimes, he mostly liked just hanging around his house.

He was kind of playful when he was relaxed, and he had a habit of throwing fries at me when I wasn't looking at him. He even built a fort of sorts around his bacon cheeseburger with them. And he hadn't been the least bit nervous since we'd indirectly talked about the action the back seat of his car had seen. At least, not that I'd noticed. So him fidgeting and staring down at his lap as he asked to see me tomorrow was not something that I really expected.

"Yeah, that'd be nice," I said, looking down at my lap as well. "My dad will be golfing most of the day so . . . maybe I could make us something for dinner, too? If you want, I mean."

"I'm completely up for that."

I laughed as I saw him smirk in the dim light from the dashboard.

"Thank you for tonight," I said, taking a deep breath and looking back down at my lap. "I really appreciate it."

"You don't have to thank me, Anna. I had a good time."

I inspected the back of my hands. "Okay. So . . . I'll see you tomorrow then."

"Do you want me to call before I come over just in case you go out or something?" He laughed. "Christina mentioned something about seeing you tomorrow."

"Ah."

"I'll call you."

"You better."

He grabbed my hand, bringing it up to his lips, and his eyes never looked away from mine the entire time as he pressed a gentle kiss against my knuckles.

"Promise."

"Then I'll talk to you tomorrow."

"Okay." I squeezed his hand before he let go and got out to open my door, my legs not altogether steady as I let him help me up.

I'd never had anyone open my door for me before. I'd never had anyone kiss my hand at the end of the night before. Hell, I'd never believed that Evan Drake would be the one to do any of that in the first place, and I'd never had the chance to really feel like maybe I wasn't such a social outcast.

Chapter Six

I jumped down the last of the stairs, bypassing my dad as I lunged for the door and looked at him over my shoulder. He held his hands up and walked back into the living room, mumbling something I was sure I didn't want to hear to begin with.

It was Sunday, and last night when I'd talked to *him* on the phone, Evan had said that he would be coming over early the next morning so that we could hang out for the whole day. We would've done something on Saturday, as we'd planned, except that Christina had held me prisoner all day yesterday and wouldn't let me out of her sight until her mother called her home at eight thirty.

"Hi," I said to him as I pulled open the door.

"Hey." He grinned, shoving his hands in his pockets. "How's it going?"

"Not too bad, I guess. You?"

"Better now."

I rolled my eyes and he laughed, pushing hair off my forehead. I turned to look as Dad yelled something at the television, and I laughed nervously and grabbed my keys.

"Going for a walk, Dad!" I yelled.

He grunted in response, and I slipped out the door.

"So, we're walking?"

"Would you rather stay in the house while my father screams at the television?"

"We could always go up to your room . . ."

"Excuse you?"

"Not for . . . I didn't mean . . ." He laughed nervously and cleared his throat, looking away. I tried not to laugh at him. "Just to hang out."

"Not a good idea," I said. "Come on."

"Where are we going?"

I hopped down the porch stairs, rounded the side of the house, and waited for him at the fence that blocked off the backyard from the neighbors that didn't exist.

"For a walk."

"In your backyard?"

"Maybe."

I pushed through the gate and looked over my shoulder to make sure that he was still following, and I smiled brightly as he closed the gate behind him.

"Is this a top secret thing, Anna?"

"It could be if you wanted it to."

"You're . . . kind of nuts, you know that?"

I reached the back end of the fence, waiting for him to catch up to me. I pulled back two of the wooden boards, motioning for him to go first.

He stared, then blinked. "We couldn't have just walked around?"

"You wanted to know if it was a top secret mission. What's a top secret mission without a secret passageway?"

"I . . . guess you have a point." He laughed, bending down and crawling through the open boards.

I followed him, replacing the boards before standing by his side and motioning to a well-worn path that I hadn't used for some time.

"Seriously, where are we going?"

"It's just a shortcut to a place where I go when I need some time to myself."

"Oh, well then." He grabbed my hand, interlocked our fingers, and waved in front of us. "By all means."

I laughed and then walked ahead of him, pulling him along with me. A few minutes and one hilarious episode later when Evan screamed like a little girl when he thought he saw a snake, we came upon the local playground. Kids were scattered on the jungle gym or the merry-go-round and ran around the slide to go down one more time, and their parents sat on the benches closest to the entrance to talk about the things their children did on a daily basis.

"You come here to think?"

I pulled him toward the entrance and led him over to a second set of unused swings in the back, letting go of his hand as I plopped into one and pushed myself off.

"There's something about hanging around kids that clears my mind. Everything is so innocent with them."

He plopped down into the swing next to me and gripped the chains as he looked around. Most of the kids had congregated around the wooden playhouse in the middle of the playground. They screamed and laughed as they ran from one end to the other using the swinging bridge.

"It was so much easier when we were kids, wasn't it?"

"It sure was." I swung as I watched a little blond-haired boy run in our direction as a redheaded girl chased him with her arms stretched out.

"I'm gonna kiss you!" she screeched, laughing.

"That's gross! Girls have cooties!" he yelled back, ducking underneath a portion of the playhouse and catching her off-guard.

"Yeah. If that was our only problem, life would be a cakewalk."

"I wonder where that expression came from," he said, looking over at me. "Who really wants to walk on a cake?"

"Well, that's like saying something is as easy as pie. Making pie from scratch is anything *but* easy."

He laughed and leaned his forehead against the chains, digging his toe into the dirt below him and pushing himself back and forth.

"Have I always been an asshole to you?" he asked.

"You remember playing together when we were younger, don't you?"

"Well, yeah, but I mean after that."

I let my toes drag in the sand as I swung. "Yeah, you have."

He reached over and grabbed my hand, once again linking our fingers together and squeezing.

"I haven't made it easy for you, have I?"

"No," I said, sitting up straight and squaring my shoulders. "But I've learned to deal with it as best I can."

"You shouldn't have to go through life like that."

"I won't have to in a few more months. I'll be off to college and starting over. It'll be different."

"Where are you going?"

"NYU."

"I applied there."

"Have you heard anything back yet?"

He looked away, toeing the dirt a little more forcefully.

"Not yet."

"What would you go for?"

"Journalism."

"You want to be a writer?" I asked.

"I'd love to be some kind of columnist or feature writer for the *New York Times*."

"That would be really cool."

"What are you going for?"

"Child psychology."

"You'd be good at that."

I smiled and ducked my head, swinging a little more forcefully and pulling him with me. He laughed and picked up the pace until we were both forced to let go for fear we'd pull the other one completely off the swing. Finally, we both slowed down, dragging our feet in the sand as we came to a stop.

"Wow! You guys went high!"

It was the kids we'd seen running around before, only now they were holding hands and staring up at us with an expression close to awe. I laughed and hopped off the swing. There was a woman with fire-engine red hair, watching closely. I pointed to the little girl and then to the swing, indicating I wanted to push her on it, and she nodded, smiling at me.

"Come on," I said to her, holding out my hand.

She grabbed my hand and abandoned the little boy, who was pouting and crossing his arms over his chest. I looked at Evan, and he jumped up, holding out his hand to the little boy, who smiled, bounced over to Evan, and grabbed his hand as well. I laughed and walked the short steps to the swing I'd just abandoned, picking the girl up to place her on the swing.

"Hold on tight, okay?"

She clapped enthusiastically and wound her little hands as far around the chains as possible, and I smiled as I walked behind her and placed my hands on her shoulders. I pushed her, and she squealed, kicking her legs out in front of her. I looked over to find Evan doing the same with the boy, who hadn't quite gotten the hang of pumping his legs to go faster. He had the basic idea, but there was no rhythm, and he was going too fast for it to make much of a difference.

"What's your name?" the little girl asked, tilting her head back to look up at me.

"Look straight ahead, sweetie, or you'll fall backwards," I instructed, placing my hands on her back and pushing her again. "My name's Anna. What's yours?"

"Ella. That's Hunter." She pointed to the little boy Evan was pushing before grabbing the chain again. "He's my boyfriend."

"Oh really?"

I stifled a laugh and saw Evan's sly smile, the little boy making gagging noises.

"Yep! Is that guy yours? He has pretty hair."

My eyes widened, and I looked back down at the top of her head, clearing my throat nervously and pushing her again.

"We're just friends, sweetie."

"Oh. Well . . . friends are good."

"Yes, friends are very good."

"Ella! Hunter! Come on! It's time to go!"

I grabbed the chains and stopped the swing as she jumped off.

"Thanks, Anna! Bye!"

"Yeah, bye!" Hunter yelled as he chased after Ella.

I looked over at Evan to find him kicking the sand, and I plopped back down into my swing and pushed myself back and forth. He slowly did the same, staring straight ahead, as he slowly swung back and forth.

"You okay?" I asked, dragging the toe of my sneakers in the dirt and looking at him.

"Yeah." He smiled at me. "I'm just thinking."

"Anything you're willing to share?"

"You're good with kids, you know?"

Looking down at my lap, I said, "Thanks. I love kids."

"I never really thought that I wanted kids."

"No?"

He stared across the park as he pushed himself off the ground and started swinging in earnest. "Too much responsibility . . . not being able to give them back to their parents when they start crying and all." He chuckled, looking over at me. "But maybe it wouldn't be so bad after all."

"You've just gotta find the right person." I shrugged and looked away, staring down at my feet as I pushed myself back. "Anything is possible then."

"You're a romantic, huh?"

"Maybe." I glanced at him and said, "Have to have something to believe in, right?"

He abruptly stopped swinging; I followed suit as he stood stiffly and walked behind me. I tensed, closed my eyes tightly, and waited for the worst to happen. His arms slid around my shoulders before I felt his breath on my ear as he bent down. I relaxed, opening my eyes and cautiously leaning back into him.

"I hope one day that you'll trust me, Anna," he whispered into my ear, his arms tightening around my shoulders. "I know it's not easy."

"I *am* trying."

"I know. So am I."

"I know that, too."

He kissed my cheek before standing, and I blushed, blinking at my feet before I felt his hands on my back, slowly pushing me forward.

"Tell me something."

"Like what?"

I crossed my ankles as he continued to push me.

"Ever snuck out before?"

"No," I snorted. "You?"

"All the time."

"Rebel."

"Maybe. Ever gotten drunk?"

"Once with Christina and Vince at her house when we were in ninth grade."

"Now who's the rebel?"

"Still you," I said, trying to hide the smile as he pushed me a little higher. "Ever not been able to talk your way out of something?"

"Only with my mom." He chuckled. "It's like she can see through me and read my mind. Ever been in love?"

"No." I sighed. "How about you?"

"I thought I was once," he said. "Turned out that not everything ends the way it's supposed to."

"What happened?"

"She broke up with me for someone else."

"Who was it?"

"She moved away a few months after."

Fourteen

I dug my heels into the dirt and turned to look at him. There was only one person that he could possibly be talking about. They had been the power couple, the king and queen of Collins Point High during freshman year until out of the blue, she showed up at school holding hands with Dane McKinley, a senior and star of the basketball team.

"Laura Crest?"

He shifted uneasily and stuck his hands in his jean pockets.

"Yeah."

"I'm sorry, Evan."

He laughed uneasily and shrugged.

"It happens."

"It sucks."

"Yeah."

I looked around to see that almost all of the kids and parents were gone. The small amount of sun we'd seen today was disappearing behind the clouds, and I grabbed his elbow, pulling him toward the abandoned jungle gym. I stopped him at the bottom and grabbed onto the sides before stepping up onto the bottom rung and climbing up to the top. After situating myself and dangling my legs in between the bars, I looked down at him.

"You coming up?"

"I guess so."

I held on to the bar I sat on and watched as he climbed up, getting settled next to me and holding on just as tightly as I was.

"What are we doing up here?"

"When you were little, did you ever think that sitting up here made you feel like the king of the world? You could see everything in the playground and watch everything everyone else was doing?"

"Well, no. I do now, though."

I giggled and leaned over to gently bump my shoulder against his.

"I'd climb up here when someone would say something mean about me," I said, looking out over the expanse of the small playground. "No one else was really brave enough to sit up on the top like this, so I felt like it was my escape."

"How long have we been . . . ?"

"Since middle school, you've all been making fun of me for my weight."

"Did you ever have someone fight for you?"

"Christina and Vince wanted to, but I wouldn't let them." I looked over at him, resting my chin on my shoulder. "It was never their battle to fight."

"It's okay to ask for help sometimes, Anna."

"I'm not dragging anyone else into this when I don't have to. Christina and Vince are their own little unit, and I wasn't going to let something like them defending me cause them to be made fun of, too. They have their own lives; this is mine."

"You can't always be this stubborn."

"Yeah." I grinned. "I am."

"I'll fight for you."

I snorted and looked away from him.

"You're going to have a hell of a time when we go to school tomorrow, Evan. Don't worry about it."

"I don't care about that."

"You won't until you're in the middle of it."

"You're really always like this?"

"Yes."

"Good to know."

"This is me, Evan. I've never compromised that for anyone, and I won't do it for you."

"I don't want you to."

I looked back over to the playhouse. A few children were running through the doorways and laughing innocently when I felt his hand covering mine. He trailed his fingers over the back of my hand and slowly worked them underneath my palm.

"You're not like anyone else," he said, sliding his fingers in between mine. "It's hard trying to pin you down."

"That's bad, I'm guessing."

"No." He laughed. "You're different and I like it."

"Mm." I looked back out over the playground.

While we'd climbed on the jungle gym and had a conversation about how stubborn I was, the kids and their parents had abandoned the playground and the sun had begun to set behind the trees. I didn't know how I didn't hear parents call their kids or the shouts and tantrums when they were told that they had to leave, but Evan and I were the only two left on the entire playground.

"I do!" Evan exclaimed, bumping my shoulder with his.

"Okay." I laughed, looking over at him once more.

He tilted his head to the side and pursed his lips.

"I mean it!"

"All right!"

"Believe me."

"I believe you!"

"Are you lying?"

"Yes."

"Anna!" he exclaimed.

"I'm being honest with you!"

"Why do you think it's so hard for me to like you?"

"Because you never have before!"

His face fell and he shifted uncomfortably, looking out toward the playhouse again.

"I've made mistakes, Anna," he said. The muscle in his jaw twitched. "This isn't one of them."

"At least, not yet, right?"

I snorted feebly and swung my legs in between the bars as I looked down at my lap.

"Hey." He removed his hand and grabbed my chin, forcing me to look over at him. "I will never consider getting to know you and being with you a mistake of any kind. Believe that, okay?"

Easier said than done.

"Yeah," I said, my voice cracking. "Okay."

"Promise?"

"Mm-hm."

"I wanna hear you say the words, Anna."

I huffed. "I promise."

"That's better."

He trailed his thumb over my bottom lip, and I looked away from him, noticing the sky had turned to a pink color.

"Doesn't this hurt your ass?" he groaned.

I looked back over at him and laughed at the expression on his face.

"I've got enough padding back there."

"Knock it off." He rolled his eyes. "Your ass is fine."

My face burned, and I looked away again, listening to him clear his throat.

"I mean it's . . ."

"Stop talking."

"Yep."

"We can get down, if you want. There's a little platform in the playhouse that we can sit on."

"What time do you need to be home?" he asked as he pulled his legs out from the spaces and climbed down.

"I don't think it really matters."

I waited until he was safely on the ground before I climbed down and jumped to the ground in front of him.

"Your dad really doesn't pay much attention, does he?"

"No." I sighed, starting toward the playhouse. "He's . . . I don't even know."

I heard his footsteps behind me. "Hey!" I yelled when he pulled on my elbow, leading me toward the big yellow slide. "What are you doing?"

He didn't say anything as he plopped down into the end of the slide, spreading his legs. I looked at him skeptically, and he laughed, rolling his eyes before grabbing my hand and gently pulling me down to rest in between them.

"I'm watching the sunset with you," he said.

My heart threatened to beat out of my chest, and I cleared my throat so that my voice wouldn't crack and give me away when I spoke. "You're one of those cuddlers, aren't you?"

He leaned forward, grabbing onto my waist and pulling me backward until my back was pressed up against his chest. He kept his arms around my waist, and I looked down, wondering if he could feel every little imperfection that my shirt was hiding—the stretch marks, the rolls, the way it was softer than what I was sure he was used to.

"I never have been much of a cuddler before," he mused. "I guess a lot of things about me are changing, huh?"

I forced myself to relax against him, placed my hands on his wrists, and leaned my head back against his chest. He felt solid. I'd never been held like this by anyone else before, and I couldn't say that I hated it. I felt safe and strangely secure.

"Do you consider it a good change or a bad one?"

"Definitely a good one, Anna." He slid his legs down beside mine, keeping me close and trapped against him. "Most definitely a good one."

"And you'll still think all of this tomorrow?"

"I wish you'd trust me," he said. "I know it's hard, and I know it's gonna take time, but I really wish that you would because I mean it."

"I'm trying to, Evan."

"I know. I *know* that. I just . . . ugh."

I laughed and rubbed his arms, watching as the pink in the sky disappeared and black overtook it.

"We're getting there."

"Progress."

"Yes." I smiled and closed my eyes, tilting my head and taking a deep breath, the scent of his musky cologne filling my nose. "Progress."

We stayed there, talking about whatever came to us until the sun completely set and I had to lead him back through the woods, laughing each time he squealed when he was *positive* something furry had brushed up against him. How he knew it was furry when he was wearing jeans was beyond me, but I was too busy laughing to even think of asking him about it.

He held onto my hand like it was a lifeline, and I swear, if I hadn't been laughing so hard as he tripped over the board to get back through the fence, probably would've dropped to his knees and kissed the ground.

Who knew *the* Evan Drake didn't like nature?

"I'm glad you think this is funny!" he barked, stalking off toward the gate.

That only made me laugh harder, and before I realized it, I was hunched over, clutching my stomach and doing my absolute best to stay on my own two feet. By the time I caught my breath and looked up, he was standing by the gate with his arms crossed over his chest.

"Are you done?"

I just wasn't used to seeing the king of the school screeching like a little girl and hopping around to avoid a branch buried underneath some leaves.

"Good." He smirked and held out a hand to me. "I'll walk you to your door."

"Now you're going to be a gentleman, huh?"

He shrugged, and I walked up to him, letting him lace our fingers together before he unlatched the gate and led me around to the front of the house. He stopped at the steps, and I made it to the second one before turning around.

"Thanks for hanging around with me today," I said, stuffing my hands into my pockets.

"Pleasure was all mine."

"Since when did you get so proper?"

"I guess you just bring it out in me."

"Mm-hm."

He grinned and stepped up on the bottom step, winding his arms around my waist and nearly pulling me off the step altogether. I closed my eyes and smiled when I felt his lips on my cheek, lingering longer than usual.

"I'll see you tomorrow," he said.

"Yeah."

"Have a good night, Anna."

"Drive safe," I managed as he stepped away from me.

"Always."

"It's gonna be rough tomorrow, you know."

He smiled. "You gonna stick around with me?"

"Of course."

He fished his keys out of his pocket. "Then it's all going to be okay."

"Yeah, I guess you're right. I'll see you later."

He smiled and turned, walking back to his car and climbing in. I stayed on the steps until he backed out and beeped the horn twice, disappearing down the road. With a smile on my face, and a little bit of hope in my heart, I turned and walked into the house.

Maybe people could change after all.

Chapter Seven

Social suicide.

That was really the only way to describe what Evan had done to himself after he was seen with me on Friday night. I was getting my books out of my locker and cringed as Steve, Brittany, Grace, and Adam cornered him at his locker. Their expressions and hand gestures gave away what they were saying.

The pointing in my direction hadn't been subtle, either.

I clutched my books tightly to my chest before turning on my heel and starting toward the science room. After sitting down on the stool, I leaned forward to cross my arms on the table and rest my chin on my hands. Focusing on the board, I found that the words began to jumble the longer I stared at them.

The door opened again, and I closed my eyes when the doorknob hit the filing cabinet behind it. The metal *clang* that resounded through the empty room echoed in my head, and I didn't open my eyes until the stool next to me scraped against the floor.

He sat down hard, all but slamming his books on the tabletop and leaning over to rest his head in his hands. His chest was heaving as he stared down at his textbook, and I sat up straight.

I wanted to say something to him, but he didn't look all that friendly right then. In fact, he looked like he wanted to rip someone's head off, and I *really* didn't want it to be mine. But this past week had been all about learning to trust and changing and chances, so backing down now would only prove that nothing had changed between us.

"Evan?" I asked, leaning back a little just in case he did lash out at me.

I jumped back when he held up a hand.

"Please don't," he said through his teeth.

I leaned forward, wrapped my arms around my books, and went back to staring at the numbers on the chalkboard. We sat in complete silence until the bell rang. I sat up straight when the rest of our class started piling in. Mr. Streeter walked in and took attendance before announcing that our homework for the night was on the board and that we had the entire class period to work on getting our projects together. Conversation immediately picked up around the room, and I slowly looked over at Evan.

"We can't use *them* for our project anymore," he said, his voice low as he kept his eyes centered on his textbook.

"Okay."

"Any ideas?"

"What about . . . " I tapped my fingertips against my chin, looking around the room as if it might have the answer to all of my questions. My eyes landed on Mr. Streeter as he sat at his desk, grading a stack of papers. "What about our teachers? And maybe we could go door-to-door? Ask our neighbors if they'd be interested in helping us out?"

"Like Girl Scouts or some stupid shit?" he snapped.

"Do you have any better ideas?" I rolled my eyes and turned back to face the front.

He groaned, and I watched from the corner of my eye as he rubbed his hands over his face.

"I'm sorry." He dropped his hands with a loud *plop* onto the table. "This isn't your fault."

"Yeah, sure." I looked down at my notebook and played with the spiral wire.

Unfortunately, it kind of was. If he hadn't chosen to be with me on Friday night instead of going to hang out with Brittany, none of this would be happening to him right now. Did it give him the right to be mean to me? No, it really didn't, but it was understandable under the circumstances.

"The teachers . . . and neighbors . . . that's a good idea. We can do that."

"Sure."

"Anna, I'm just . . . they're . . . I . . . " He groaned again and rapped his fists lightly on the desk. "Please don't be mad at me, okay?"

"I'm not. I'm just . . ." I sighed. "I'm not." He sucked in a deep breath. "Let's just work on the paper, okay? We've got enough information to at least start on it."

"Yeah, that's good."

I pulled the papers out of my notebook and handed him half of them. We spent the rest of the class, asking each other questions about things we thought could be helpful. When the bell rang, I took the papers Evan offered me and shoved them back into my notebook.

"I have practice tonight," he said as he slammed his books closed and stood up. "I'll come over afterward, all right?"

"Yeah, that's fine."

"I'll see you at lunch."

He slid off the stool, smiled humorlessly and said, "I, uh . . ."

"Yeah, that's fine," I said. "I'll see you at lunch."

"Thanks," he mumbled before turning on his heel and walking out.

I puffed out my cheeks and followed him. I felt a little guilty about everything that was happening to him. Granted, I liked spending time with him, but I didn't enjoy the way he'd seemed forced to give up everything he'd known just because of me.

". . . don't know who she thinks she is."

I caught the tail end of a conversation before I kept walking.

"It will never work out with them. He's got to be just using her to get a good grade on this project."

I held my books tighter to my chest, keeping my eyes focused on my locker door as my heart beat rapidly in my chest.

"Maybe he's just sick. I mean, really, Evan doesn't do girls like her."

I walked a little faster, making it to my locker in record time and shoving my human physiology stuff inside. I did my best to block everyone else out and hurried to grab the books I needed for my English class before I slammed my locker shut.

"He's only using her. I know it."

I practically ran to the classroom and plopped down in my seat. Kyle came walking toward me, and I held my breath when I saw his eyes focus on me. He'd been sitting in the seat in front of me all year, and aside from a few polite smiles, he'd never acknowledged me before.

"You okay, Anna?" he asked, standing beside his seat.

I blinked at him, my breath whooshing out of my lungs. Just because

I'd been halfheartedly expecting it didn't make it any less shocking when he spoke to me. He might've tried to shield me from my locker last week, but it was still weird that he was talking to me where people could clearly see and hear him.

"Hello?"

He waved a hand in front of my face, and I jumped back.

"Sorry," he said, sitting down.

"I'm fine, thank you," I said to the back of his head.

A few more months, Anna. You can make it through a few more months.

~*~

I slid onto the bench at the lunch table where I usually sat with Christina and Vince and leaned back against the wall. I pulled my legs up to my chest and watched the door anxiously.

The comments hadn't gotten any better. Everyone was apparently talking about how Evan was so sick or just trying to get a good grade or feeling sorry for me after all these years. I was ready to jump out of my skin. Everything I had forewarned him about was happening, and though even the littlest comments stung, at least I was semi-used to them. Evan wasn't, and I was worried how he would handle this particular brand of attention.

He had more to lose than I did, and he was losing it at an alarmingly rapid pace.

I picked at my bottom lip, staring at the end of the bench as I waited for Christina and Vince to show up while trying to calm the nerves I felt when I thought of Evan sitting with us.

Would Christina and Vince be okay with it him sitting here? Would they be mad that I hadn't asked them if it was okay? Would it matter?

I moaned and buried my head in my hands, closing my eyes and taking deep breaths as I listened to the normal clatter around the cafeteria.

"You going to make it, Anna?"

I looked up when I heard Vince's voice. I dropped my arms onto my knees and forced a smile as I dropped my feet to the floor.

Looking between the two of them, I said, "Uh, Evan's going to sit with us today."

"I figured." Vince shrugged, plopping down onto the bench and immediately tearing open the top of his bagged lunch. "He's been getting hell all day."

I groaned again and dramatically flung my arms onto the tabletop, burying my face in the crook of my elbow.

"What? Something I said?" he asked around the food in his mouth.

"You're lucky you're cute," Christina said with sarcasm.

"You know it."

"You're both sickening," I said with a huff, lifting my head and resting my chin on my forearm.

"You love us." Christina grinned as she pulled open her own bagged lunch. "Otherwise you wouldn't put up with us."

I furrowed my brow and watched the two of them eat their lunches.

"Can I ask a question?" I asked, sitting up straight and looking at the doorway.

Where the hell was Evan?

"Always."

"You two are always hanging out with me, yet you're still considered popular." I tapped my fingertips against the tabletop. "Why do you think it's such a big deal with Evan?"

"Evan's been the golden boy," Vince said, shoving a potato chip into his mouth and pointing at me with his greasy finger. "He's never stepped out of their comfort zone."

"Ugh. Could you finish chewing before you speak?" I asked, tilting my head to the side.

He scowled at me and grabbed another chip, jamming it into his mouth. Christina rolled her eyes and gently bumped her shoulder against his. "We never really participated in their stupid shit," she said with a wave of her hand over her shoulder. "We've always done whatever we wanted and never bothered with whatever they were doing when it didn't have to deal the squad or the team." She flicked a crumb off the table and smiled at me. "We've always been just on the outskirts and never got involved with their personal lives. Evan did."

It made sense; Evan had been with the in-crowd for a very long time. Christina and Vince had always been on the outskirts—popular because Vince was a football player and Christina was a cheerleader—but had never really participated in the crap that came with it. They were genuinely nice people that kept to themselves and associated with the others when they had to, nothing more, nothing less.

I looked down at my hands and then jumped when a tray slammed down on the table next to me as Evan climbed onto the bench and sat down in much the same fashion as he had that morning in human physiology.

"Hey," he said, grabbing his fork and stabbing at what was supposed to be coleslaw.

"Hey, dude." Vince smacked Evan on the arm. "How's it going?"

"Ouch, Anna!" Vince jerked back and winced, reaching down to rub his leg.

I glared at him, silently telling him to shut up.

"Peachy," Evan grumbled. "Fucking peachy."

I looked over at him briefly before placing my hands in my lap and looking over at Christina.

"Don't you eat?" Evan asked me.

"Not school food."

He grunted, going back to poking his food with his fork. "Smart. Tastes like ass, anyway."

"You want to do dinner or something later this week?" Christina asked.

I smiled gratefully at her as we filled the awkward silence with dinner plans. Christina, Vince, and I did most of the talking. Evan grunted and said a few things here and there, but for the most part, he kept stabbing his food. I wanted to touch him, put my hand on his back, or grab his hand under the table and squeeze it just to reassure him, but I wasn't sure of the reaction I'd get, and God knew I didn't want to be on the receiving end of his wrath ever again.

We all stood up when the bell rang and walked over to the garbage cans. They threw their things away before Vince and Christina said their goodbyes, joined hands, and walked out of the room.

Smiling awkwardly I said, "I'll see you later."

"Anna."

"Yeah?"

He grabbed my hand and pulled me back to him, leaning in and brushing his lips against my forehead. I closed my eyes and took a deep breath, the small amount of contact we had drowned out the immediate rise in voices in the room.

"I'll walk with you," he said, gently squeezing my hand before dropping it and shoving his hands into his pockets as he stepped back.

I opened my eyes.

"Okay."

"I uh . . . I just . . . ," he stuttered, reaching up to rub the back of his neck. "I need . . ."

"Stop," I said. "Just walk me to my locker, Evan."

I turned on my heel, starting out of the room and doing my best to ignore everyone else.

Why had he done that? It didn't make any sense. Not that I minded, really. I just didn't understand any of it, especially since he'd seemed so embarrassed and almost guilty about if afterward.

I sighed heavily and crossed my arms over my chest, aware of him walking beside me as we rounded the corner and started toward my locker. When we got there, he stood behind me as if he were standing guard.

"Don't you need your books?" I turned to look at him.

"Study hall."

"You didn't have to do that, you know."

"What?"

"*That*." I pointed toward the cafeteria, waving my hand around in emphasis.

"I wanted to."

"And you regretted it."

"Excuse me?"

"You just . . ." I huffed in frustration and turned away from him, grabbing my books and slamming my locker door closed. "You seemed like you . . . you can tell me the truth, Evan."

"Anna, the only thing I've got left right now is you." He grabbed my shoulders, and I flinched. He immediately dropped his hands. "It was just a . . . a thank you, I guess."

"For what?" I asked.

"For giving me another chance." He dropped his hands to his sides. "For sticking with me today."

I raised my hand, ready to place it on his cheek before I snatched it back and wrapped my arms around my books.

"I told you I would."

He looked up at me, a piece of hair falling into his face. "Seeing is believing."

"Tell me about it."

His mouth twitched. "I'll see you after practice."

"I'll be there."

"You'd better be."

I chuckled and he grinned, leaning in and kissing my cheek before I had time to react. He was awfully good at that.

"See you," he whispered before striding off down the hallway with his hands shoved in his pockets.

I watched him until the bell rang and then took off in the direction of my economics class. Well, I knew today would be interesting.

~*~

That night Evan came over, and when I opened the door, I was stunned by his appearance. He had a black eye, a split lip, a cut on his cheek, and a bandage on his chin. He looked like he wanted to punch something.

"What . . . ?"

"Don't," he said, taking a step toward me.

I moved out of the way to let him in, upset when I saw the slight limp in his step.

"Evan."

"I'm not talking about it."

"You can't—"

"Anna," he snapped, turning and wincing. "I'm fine."

"It shows," I said sarcastically, finally closing the door.

"It's practice. What did you really expect?"

"You've never come over looking like *this* before!"

"Yeah, well . . ."

He mumbled something under his breath as he hobbled his way toward the kitchen. I followed him, listening as he took a sharp breath and fell into one of the chairs at the table. He shouldered off his backpack and dropped it to the floor, muttering something else that I couldn't hear.

"Do you want something for your eye?" I asked, fidgeting.

"Ice would be great." He sighed, leaning his elbow on the table and placing his forehead in his palm.

I walked over to the freezer and grabbed the same ice pack I'd used for my wrist, wrapping it in a paper towel before handing it to him. I sat down in the chair next to him and rested my arms on the table as he pressed the pack against his eye. He hissed in pain, and I cringed.

"Was it—"

"Not talking about it," he interrupted, holding up his hand.

"It was because of me," I whispered.

He didn't say anything and confirmed my suspicions. If I hadn't felt bad before, his silence made me feel ten times worse.

"Let's just do our homework so that this day can be over with." He shifted uncomfortably and dropped the ice pack to grab his bag. "I *need* this day to be over with."

I stood and grabbed my bag from the front hallway.

It's funny how things can change in a matter of days. I never would've imagined that Evan Drake would give up his popularity and damage his reputation because of someone like me.

I walked back into the kitchen and dropped my bag on the floor by his chair. Carefully, I placed my hands on his shoulders and leaned down to kiss the top of his head, his hair tickling my nose and making me smile a little. He reached up and squeezed my hand carefully.

"Come on." He tugged on my hand. "We've got homework to get done."

I squeezed his shoulder and kicked my bag over to my chair. I felt like hell that this happened because of me, but it didn't mean that I didn't appreciate it.

Chapter Eight

I hadn't known the meaning of hell until Evan was ostracized from his group of so-called "friends." I was used to the name-calling and being picked on, and yes, it had increased tenfold, but Evan was not used to any of it. There had been more than one occasion when I'd had to find new ways to keep him occupied and get his mind off everything they were saying; it hadn't been easy. There were only so many stories I could tell him about my younger days when things were good at home before he stopped laughing.

Evan never took it out on me, though. He'd promised that he wouldn't and he hadn't. I didn't trust him completely, but I trusted him more than I had a week ago.

We'd obviously gotten close through all of this, and it made my heart beat faster every time he'd randomly grab my hand while we were working on something, keeping his eyes focused on whatever was in front of him as he rubbed his thumb on my palm.

He had his moments, of course, when he'd get aggravated about everything everyone was saying, and I didn't make it any better when I'd looked at him as if he had three heads. I tended to forget that he was new to the whole social outcast thing, and he tended to forget that this was nothing new to me. When we both realized what we were doing, we found some way to distract ourselves and forget about everything that had happened during the day, whether we watched a movie, listened to music, or just talked about something completely off topic.

Fourteen

While I still felt horrible that all of this was happening because he chose to befriend me and stick up for me when his other friends still thought I had the plague, it was nice to have someone else to talk to. I could talk to Christina, and she'd do her best to understand and comfort me, but it was ten times different with Evan. Christina had never had to worry about being accepted or trying to fit in—it was just something that had come naturally to her. She was the girl that fit in everywhere with everyone, and while she was my best friend and I loved her dearly, I envied her that. He *had* changed and for once, it was nice to be proven wrong.

On Thursday, we were sitting on the floor in my living room, taking a break from our project and working on our English homework when he looked up and stared at me. I sat at one end of the coffee table, and he was at the other, shifting and grumbling things I couldn't understand for the most part.

"Yes?" I asked, not taking my eyes off the weathered copy of *The Tell-Tale Heart* opened in my lap.

"Are you ever going to let me kiss you?" he blurted.

I stopped reading, shocked. "I wasn't aware that you wanted to."

My voice shook a little, and it felt as if my heart had just leapt into my throat. That was not at all what I'd been expecting to hear from him.

Okay. Play it cool, Anna. Keep it together.

"Seriously?"

"Your mom's been watching *Grey's* reruns again, hasn't she?"

"Anna," he snapped.

I dog-eared the page I was reading and noticed that my hands were shaking. I closed the book and looked up at him.

"Yes?"

"I'm being serious."

"And I seriously wasn't aware that you wanted to, Evan."

"Well . . . I do."

"I didn't, uh . . . I wasn't . . ."

I felt like I was going to explode—but in an extremely good way. Trying to keep my wits about me while I was jumping up and down on the inside as a little girl that had just got her first bike was not easy.

"You never . . . I just . . . ugh." He groaned, fidgeting. "You always just . . . I never know what you're thinking."

"About what?"

"About me!" he exclaimed, looking up at me again. "Do you want

C.M. Smith

more with me, or do you just want to be friends? I never know what to do with you."

"What do *you* want with me, Evan?" My heart was once again beating through my chest.

I'd done my best not to hope for anything more with him. I'd seen the side of him that I thought could still exist. While I may have wanted more, may have wanted him to look at me in a different light, I wasn't going to push the little bit of luck that I'd had so far.

One date, a week's worth of working on a project for school and getting to know him, had only left me with the hope that we were *friends*. I'd already ruined his reputation, and the majority of his friends weren't talking to him; I wasn't hoping for a miracle.

"I want . . . more," he finally admitted.

My heart fluttered.

"You do?"

"I thought you got that."

"You've understandably been all over the place this week, Evan. I didn't know *what* to think about anything."

"Sorry." He shifted uneasily on the floor. "I just . . . this is *hard*." He chuckled and looked down at the coffee table. "I'm not used to this."

I bit the inside of my cheek and set the book on the table before standing. I stretched briefly before walking over to him and sitting down next to him. "Sorry."

"You don't have anything to apologize for." He sighed. "I wish you'd stop."

"It's because of me that you're in this predicament."

"If it weren't for you, we wouldn't be like this, either. I'd take this over them any day."

I barely contained the grin that wanted to crack my face, and he laughed, grabbing my hand. He pulled it into his lap, twisting our fingers together and looking down at them. He trailed his hand over the back of mine, slowly dragging his fingers down over my wrist and gently over the area where my bruises were almost non-existent at this point.

"I can't apologize enough for this," he whispered.

"Hey, come on," I said, trying to pull my hand away from him. "It's over and done with; you've been forgiven."

"I still did it, Anna. To you. For no other reason than because I was having a bad day and you were . . . nothing to me at that point."

I involuntarily flinched, and he looked over at me quickly. His right eye was still bruised, and while the bandage from his chin was gone, there was still a mark that stood out against his skin.

"You know everything's different now, don't you?" he asked, his voice almost frantic as he tightened his grip on my hand. "You're so much more than that now. You know that, right?"

"Okay, my hand?" I tried to pull away from him. "Not made of steel."

He let go of my hand, leaning forward to rest his elbows on the coffee table.

"Can I ask you something?" I asked, pulling my hand back into my lap and looking down as I fidgeted.

"Mm-hm."

"Am I worth all of this to you? Losing your friends, ruining your reputation?"

"Do you really have to ask me that?" he asked.

"I just want to make sure, Evan. You still have time to make it right with everyone. You can go back to school tomorrow, and everything can go back to the way it used to be."

"No, it can't." He sat back and turned to face me, his hands resting on my thigh.

I did my best to concentrate on what he was saying.

"Everything is different now, and I wouldn't want that to change. You *are* worth it to me."

I rested my hands over his. "All right."

"Your hand okay?"

I held up my hand and flexed my fingers for him. He laughed and grabbed it, pulling my palm to his lips.

"So," he began, lowering my hand to his lap again, "I have free rein to kiss you now, right?"

Stay cool, stay cool, stay cool.

"If you'd like to, yes."

"You've been kissed before, right?"

"I was not a complete shut-in."

"I just wanted to make sure." He held up his hand. "I could've made it all fancy if you hadn't."

"Oh yeah? How?"

"I could've brought you flowers or done something really cheesy like walking you up to your front door after a date and being all awkward there."

"You won't be all awkward now?"

"Maybe a little." He chuckled and slowly leaned forward. I glanced at his mouth and licked my lips.

"You going to kiss me now?"

"Mm-hm." He smiled at me. "Is that okay?"

"I suppose so."

"Don't sound so excited."

"Would you like me to jump up and down?" I said, his nose brushing against mine.

Aside from wanting him to finally kiss me, jumping up and down was exactly what I felt like doing, to be perfectly honest.

"A little fanfare would be nice, yes."

I laughed and placed my hands on his cheeks.

"Just kiss me already, will you?"

"If you insist," he whispered as he tilted his head and pressed his lips against mine.

I closed my eyes as he gently sucked my top lip into his mouth. His lips were so soft, and they felt so much better against mine than I thought they ever would. He placed his hands on each side of my neck, his fingers tangling in my hair as he ran his thumbs up and down my throat. Small fireworks went off behind my eyes, and I couldn't fight my smile. I trailed my hands from his cheeks down to his chest, fisting my hands in his shirt as he pressed his lips more forcefully against mine. I scraped my teeth along his bottom lip, my heart picking up speed when a breathy moan vibrated against my lips. I was doing that to him—he did that because of the things that *I* did. I wanted to get up and start dancing around, chanting, *"I'm kissing Evan, I'm kissing Evan!"* but the actual act was a whole lot better than just boasting about it. I'd hoped and imagined this for so long, and now it was finally happening. I wasn't dreaming and this wasn't a joke. He pulled away slowly, kissing my top lip a few more times. He sat back down next to me, and I looked over at him, licking my lips as he did the same. My heart was still beating rapidly, and I could feel that my cheeks were flushed, but I didn't even care. The small smile I saw on his face made the one I had double, and I felt like I wanted to bounce around the room with how freaking excited I was.

"Deal breaker?" I asked when he continued to sit there in silence.

"What?" he asked, immediately looking over at me. "Fuck no."

"You were quiet."

"Thinking of . . . everything I've ever said to you." He looked away. "Everything everyone's ever said to you."

I sighed and carefully reached up to thread my hand through his hair. He grunted and leaned into my hand, his eyes closing.

"You've gotta let it go," I whispered.

"Have you?"

"That's my problem."

He grunted again. He placed his hands on my waist and twisted me around so that my back was to him, his legs suddenly on each side of me as he pulled me against his chest and wrapped his arms around me. He rested his chin on my shoulder, and I carefully leaned into him, resting my hands on his forearms.

"You're probably the strongest person I've ever met," he said. "And I'm sorry that it's taken me all this time to see it."

"You've gotta stop apologizing."

"I was and probably still am one of the biggest assholes in our entire school, and I made your life hell for a very long time. I have a *lot* to apologize for."

"You know something?" I asked, turning to look back at him.

"I know nothing."

I rolled my eyes.

"You're kind of making up for everything you've ever put me through right now. You're probably very well aware that I've had this thing for you since freshman year and—"

"Whoa, what?" he interrupted.

I ducked my head a little and wringed my hands together.

"Yeah."

"Seriously?"

"You've *got* to stop watching television with your mother."

"And *you've* got to stop deflecting my questions." He reached up his hand to frame my face. "Freshman year?"

I fidgeted.

"After everything I . . . you still . . ."

"I wanted to think the best of you because I saw something when you were with your family that I didn't see in school."

"And I just . . . I said . . . I did . . . all of that . . . all this time . . ."

"Full sentences, please," I said.

He dropped his hands from my face, staring over my shoulder, and I was positive that I'd said and done something wrong. I closed my eyes tightly and was two seconds away from bolting up the stairs and locking myself in my room until graduation. I could do everything from home; there would be no logical reason for me to go back to school for more than getting my homework. Right?

"Why did you help me?" he whispered.

"What?"

"Why did you even bother helping me that day when I dropped my papers? Why did you? Anna, I don't . . . I can't believe that . . ."

His arms were around me again, pulling me back to his chest, and he rested his chin on my shoulder.

"I was sure there was still some of that little boy I used to play with hiding inside of you somewhere."

"And there wasn't until a few days ago." His arms tightened around me, and he moved his legs in closer, keeping me nestled in tight against him. "Why did you ever give me another chance?"

"Because you gave me a flower."

When he laughed, he sounded on the verge of being hysterical, and I was slightly worried.

"I gave you a flower and you . . ."—he buried his nose in my neck —". . . a flower got me here."

"More or less."

"I have never been more thankful for my mother's obsession with orchids than I am right now, let me tell you. Jesus Christ, Anna, I will spend . . . however long you want me to, making up for everything you've been through, everything I've put you through."

"You don't have to."

"Yes, yes, I fucking do."

"Evan, it's not—"

"Anna, you're beautiful"—I snapped my mouth shut and blinked rapidly at the television in front of me—"and everyone in that entire school is a fucking idiot."

"Not . . . not everyone is . . ."

"Majority of them," he said with his lips pressed against my neck. "You were right, and I was wrong about everything. We had no right. We had no reason." He trailed his lips up to my ear and pressed a gentle kiss against it. "I'm so sorry."

"Will you do me a favor?" I asked.

"Anything."

"Stop apologizing for stuff that's over and done with."

"Anna, I feel like—"

"I know how you feel. You've told me, and you've apologized, which is something that no one else has ever bothered to do before." I placed my hands on his forearms again, sucking in a deep breath. "That means a lot to me."

"You really don't ask for all that much, do you?"

"Just the world." I grinned back at him.

He laughed, swaying us from side-to-side.

I relaxed against him and closed my eyes, squeezing his arm. Despite the conversation we'd just had, I felt content. For once, I didn't feel stressed-out or worried about every little thing that I knew was right around the corner, and it was nice to relax.

At least, until my father opened the front door.

"Oh, no." I opened my eyes.

Dad was staring at us, completely immobile with one hand on the doorknob and the other gripping his keys. Evan immediately moved away from me, and I groaned, leaning forward so that he could presumably back as far away from me as possible. I blushed and stood, Evan doing the same.

"Evan, I think it's about time that you went home," my dad said, his eyes trained on me.

"Yeah, I'm uh . . . I'm going."

I turned to Evan, and he offered me a small smile and said, "I'll see you tomorrow."

He gathered his books and shoved them back into his bag before slinging it over his shoulder. He looked at me, his gaze flicking to my father once, and he leaned in and kissed my cheek. My dad cleared his throat, and I glared at him before following Evan to the front door as he bolted out of the house. He waved over his shoulder before practically diving into his car. I closed the door and crossed my arms over my chest, staring at my dad's feet and waiting for whatever it was that he had to say.

"What was that, Arianna?"

I ground my teeth together. "That was me and Evan."

"What's going on with you two?"

"We're—" I suddenly realized a little too late that I had no idea what was going on. We hadn't put a label on whatever we were, and I wasn't going to presume that he was my boyfriend because, really, that was almost laughable. Even after the kiss and the confession, I didn't know. And I'd never asked because at that moment, it hadn't really mattered. "We're hanging out."

"You hang out with all of your friends that way?"

"What other friends?" I asked through my teeth.

"That couple you hang out with." I slowly ran my tongue along my bottom teeth, and he waved me off. "Doesn't matter. You are not to be alone with him."

"Oh, so *now* you want to be my protector? *Now* you're concerned about what I do?"

"I'm always concerned about what you do, Anna, I'm your dad! It's what I do!"

"Yeah? Well you sure as hell don't act like it most of the time! This is the most you've said to me since mom died five years ago!"

"I can't . . . don't you—" he stuttered, obviously flustered.

"You've got more interest in that damn television than you do me! You don't ask me how my day was, you didn't even come to check on me last week. I didn't know you were home until Evan said that you'd let him in. I'm just a pain in your ass, and I'm tired of it!"

"You know that's not true. You're my daughter and I love you. I'm doing the best I can right now, Anna! It's not easy!"

I stared at him, at a complete loss for words and wanting to be anywhere but in the same room with him.

"I have to go," I said, turning and pulling the door open.

"Where?" he called out as I stepped onto the porch.

"I don't know. A run, I guess."

"It's dark out."

Thank you for pointing out the obvious, father. *Guess I'm just too damn stupid to see for myself.*

"I hadn't noticed. Thanks for the update," I retorted.

I pulled the door closed and took off in the opposite direction of where I usually ran. My head was everywhere, and not one single thought made any sense to me. Before I realized it, I was standing at the end of the Drake's driveway, breathing heavily and staring up at the big white house on the hill.

Why had I come here? I wasn't sure how I got here. I knew where he lived; everyone knew where the Drakes lived, but still. He was probably going to think I was stalking him because hell, I just had to go and tell him that I liked him that entire time, didn't I? Just because he hadn't seemed upset about it, didn't mean he wouldn't be now. Maybe he'd changed his mind already. I found myself pacing up and down at the base of his driveway like a caged animal, trying to figure out what I was to him.

I scoffed to myself. I had told him to stick me in a cage at one point, hadn't I?

Just turn around and go home, Anna. Why is he going to want to see you right now? Go home, deal with your father, and you'll see Evan tomorrow, you over-dramatic pain in the butt.

"Anna?"

I jumped and stopped pacing. Evan was jogging down his driveway toward me. While I'd been lost in my head, the entire front lawn had lit up like a damn Christmas display, and I was amazed that I hadn't seen it.

Well, there goes the idea of leaving.

"Everything okay? How'd you get here?" he asked as he reached me, looking over the top of my head.

"I, uh . . ." I licked my lips and looked down, finally noticing that my legs were tingling. "I ran."

"You ran . . ."—I shrugged—"from your house."

"Yeah, so?"

"Anna, that's five miles."

"Oh." I laughed nervously before directing my gaze over his shoulder.

"What happened?"

"I don't . . . I really don't know." I marveled at the realization that I really didn't know what had happened after he'd left. My father and I had gotten into a fight, but how had it escalated to me leaving? "My dad and I had a fight and I left."

"Okay," he said, pulling me into his arms. "A bad fight?"

I snorted against his chest and buried my nose into his shirt.

"Are there any fights that could be classified as good, Evan?"

"I don't know. Maybe." He tightened his arms around me and rubbed my back.

Something seemed to click, and I groaned, backing away from him. Not only was I a disgusting, sweaty mess, but I was also sure that I'd probably disrupted whatever he and his family might've been doing.

"You're probably busy, aren't you? Or eating dinner . . . or doing something else that I interrupted, and I just . . . I'm sorry. I'll just go, okay?"

"Did I say I was busy?" he asked, grabbing my hand and pulling me back to him. "You're fine."

"How'd you even know I was here?"

"Mom went on this security kick about a year ago and insisted that we get a camera installed at the end of the driveway for some stupid reason. There's such a high crime rate in Collins Point, you know?"

I snorted again and relaxed enough to wrap my arms around his waist, closing my eyes and burying my face in his chest again. He didn't seem to mind my sweat, and I wasn't one to look a gift horse in the mouth. I needed comfort, and if he was willing to provide it for me, I wasn't turning him away.

"Do you want to come in and relax for a little while?" he asked after a few minutes.

"I don't think . . . your family . . ."

"Knows all about you." He grabbed my shoulders and gently pushed me back from him. "They want to meet you. Mom was even saying that we should have you over for dinner sometime next week."

I blinked at him.

"I'm not a secret and I refuse to be yours," he whispered.

I stared at him as my eyes watered before embracing him.

"Was that . . . did I . . . was that not something I should've said?"

"You remembered," I cried, curling my hands into the back of his shirt.

"Well . . . yes."

"I . . . I didn't think . . . I . . ."

"Okay, come inside, Anna."

"Not like this!" I cried. "I can't meet your family like this."

"All right," he said, rubbing my back. "Well . . . let's go sit down, okay? There's a bench right over here."

"Okay." I moved away from him, sniffling and letting him lead me to a stone bench by the porch. I plopped down onto it and did my best to calm down, drying the last of my tears with my shirt. He sat next to me and wrapped his arm around my shoulders, pulling me against him. I leaned against his body.

"I'm sorry," I said after a few minutes.

He kissed the top of my head and placed one hand on my thigh, trailing his other hand through my hair. "Don't be."

"I didn't mean to come here. I just . . . I just left, and I ended up here, and I'm sure I ruined your entire night with this and—"

"Stop," he said, interrupting me. "It's fine, Anna."

"What are we, Evan?" I asked after a few moments of silence.

"I told my family that you were my girlfriend," he said. "I thought that's what the whole purpose of the conversation this afternoon was about."

"I wasn't sure. We never said . . ."

"Is that what you want with me?"

"Yeah."

"All right then." He kissed the top of my head again. "Do you wanna talk about it?"

"I thought we just did."

"You know what I mean."

I sighed and closed my eyes.

"He hasn't been the same since Mom died." I opened my eyes and looked down at his lap. "He hasn't been involved with anything I've done since then, and I kind of just exploded on him tonight about it. It just . . ." I chuckled halfheartedly.

"I'm anything but invisible at school, and I come home to . . . silence and disconnection, and then he tells me that I can't be alone with you without giving me any real reason. I couldn't . . ." I turned, burying my nose in his shoulder and squeezing my eyes shut. "I just couldn't deal with it."

"It's been a rough week."

I snorted, and he laughed and wrapped his arms around me.

"Understatement of the year."

"Maybe even the century," he agreed.

I sighed. "I should probably get home."

"Come inside real quick," he said. "Meet my family. I'll drive you home."

"You don't have to—"

"You're not running five miles back in the dark, Anna. That's completely out of the question."

I smiled against his shirt, sat up, and kissed his cheek.

"Thank-you."

"Anytime."

Chapter Nine

I damn near skipped into school the next morning. I ignored all the looks I'd been dealing with all week and the aching muscles in my legs from running five miles the night before and walked straight to my locker as if I didn't have a care in the world.

I wasn't even concerned about the fact that my dad had grounded me for a week. I was only allowed to see Evan to work on our project, and it either had to be when he was home or I'd have to go over to Evan's house where his mother could watch us. Apparently, everyone knew that she worked from home except for me. Regardless, I didn't wholly regret the things I'd said to my father because, for the most part, they were true. I'd take the grounding rather than apologize for the things I'd meant.

But I'd met Evan's family. He'd introduced me to them as his girlfriend, and they'd seemed genuinely happy to meet me. His younger sister, Sherri, who was attending a gifted art school in Albany, which I envied her for, was the epitome of energy, and it was obvious to see that she and Evan adored each other. His parents, Zack and Amy, were extremely nice, welcoming, and highly amusing. When they'd offered to whip out the baby pictures and started talking about some of Evan's interesting bath time rituals from his younger days, Evan practically jumped on his mother and clamped his hands over her mouth.

I saw what I'd always imagined when I'd caught glimpses of them out and around town in the past; he was more relaxed and comfortable than he'd ever been in school. He was joking, laughing and enjoying every little thing anyone said—well, minus the bath and baby pictures thing—and it was really nice to see after the week he'd had.

He'd driven me home half an hour after I'd arrived and was about an inch away from kissing me goodnight when the front door opened and my father walked out. He leaned against doorjamb of the door with his arms crossed over his chest and looked annoyed. So I'd settled with a kiss on the cheek and made it into the house in enough time for my dad to tell me that I was grounded before he disappeared into the living room for the rest of the night. I'd merely gone in there to get my books before I went up to my room and finished my homework, going to bed early.

Despite that, I was still in a good mood because when I opened my eyes this morning, I realized that I got to see my *boyfriend* at school. For the first time in longer than I could remember, I was actually excited about having to go to that prison, disguised as a high school.

I shoved my bag into my locker, looked wistfully at the dried orchid I had hanging off the hook in the back, and grabbed my books for human physiology. When an arm wrapped around my waist, I jumped and then tensed, preparing myself for the worst before I felt him drop a kiss to the top of my head.

"Good morning, girlfriend," he said.

I smiled and closed my locker door, turning and looking up at him.

"Good morning, boyfriend."

"How's it going?"

"Better."

"Compared to?"

"I'm grounded." I shrugged and his face fell. "We can only work on our project if we're being supervised."

"Supervised?"

I rolled my eyes. "Yeah, I don't know what the big damn deal is."

He sighed heavily and leaned forward to rest his forehead against mine. I wasn't able to bite back the grin that spread across my face, and he chuckled.

"What has you so happy?"

"You," I answered honestly.

"Is that right?"

"Mm-hm."

"What about me?"

"Fishing for compliments, are we?" I asked.

He laughed and stood up straight, his arms back around my waist as he backed me up against the locker and looked down at me.

"No more than usual."

I saw a flash go off from the corner of my eye before I heard, "You two might actually rival the two of us."

Kyle and Ashley—with her ever-present camera hanging around her neck—stood behind us, both of them looking a lot more relaxed and comfortable than they'd been the last time I'd seen them. I felt a little cautious around them because, to be honest, I still didn't know if they'd been a part of the locker incident. It had seemed like they'd tried to keep me from seeing it, but there were too many questions still bouncing around in my mind to feel completely comfortable around them.

"I don't think that's possible," Evan said casually. He kept his arms around my waist and leaned against the lockers next to me, linking his fingers on my hip.

"Yeah, well, you know how we are," Kyle said, draping an arm around Ashley's shoulders.

"*We?* No, that's all you," she disagreed, pinching his side.

He yelped, and I looked on in thinly veiled amusement.

"I've never heard any complaints!"

"How can you when you won't let me breathe?" she asked innocently, batting her eyelashes at him.

I laughed, and Kyle pouted as he crushed Ashley against his chest.

She scoffed and pushed him away from her. "Where are Christina and Vince?" Evan asked.

"They both have study hall first period, so they got their parents to write them a note to get out of it."

"Lucky bastards."

I laughed and agreed with him.

"So," Ashley began, eyeing Kyle as he stood next to me, glaring at his girlfriend, "are you two going to Steve's party tonight?"

"Uh . . ." I looked over at Evan. "I can't."

"And I probably won't." He sighed.

"How come?" Kyle asked, making his way back to Ashley's side.

"Have you not been here all week? I'm not exactly talking to the same people anymore."

"You're talking to us." Ashley shrugged, eyeing Kyle as he slid his arm around her shoulders. "You've always talked to us. Nothing's changed there."

"Why can't you go?" Kyle asked, his gaze focusing on me.

Stepping closer to Evan, I said, "I'm grounded."

"Oh, well . . . that sucks." Then he got a mischievous look on his face. "Do you want to go? I'm sure I can concoct a plan to get you out of the house."

"You are *not* going where I think you're going," Ashley immediately said, pointing at him.

"What? Babe, come on! I hardly ever get to wear my ski mask!" Kyle whined, going so far as to stomp his foot.

"Damn good reason for it, too."

"How long have you two been married now?" I asked, laughing a little and forcing myself to relax.

"Too damn long!" Ashley exclaimed, rolling her eyes. "He's like a damn dog with a bone, you know. He can't just let things go."

"Think so, huh?" he asked.

"Oh Jesus," Evan said, leaning in and burying his nose in my neck. He looked up after placing a small kiss against my shoulder, resting his chin there. "Was there a reason you wanted to know about the party?"

"Come with us," Kyle said. "Come on, Ev, it's the last one before the big game! It's the last time we'll get a chance to relax before Coach tries to kill us during practice."

"I think my invitation was revoked."

I looked down at my feet, hugging my books to my chest. He still would've been invited had I not been in the picture. He stood up straight, his hands still linked around my hips.

"Fuck him. I just re-invited you."

"I really don't want to deal with his bullshit."

"It'll give me an excuse to smack him around a bit." Kyle shrugged. "Come on, dude."

"You should go," I said.

He looked down at me, clearly surprised.

"What?"

"You should go," I said again, chuckling nervously. "You've had a rough week and getting out with some friends is probably what you need."

"But they're not my friends anymore. Not really . . ."

"We're your friends, dammit!" Ashley exclaimed, tapping her foot on the linoleum. "We invited you. You're coming, and I don't want to hear another damn word about it!"

"I don't want to go without Anna," he said.

I turned to him, leaning against the lockers so that I was facing him. He tightened his arms around me and pulled me close, smirking.

"I can't go, Evan. And I probably can't see you at all this weekend unless you really want to spend all of it working on the project." He grunted. "So go to the party."

"Why can't we just go somewhere else?" he asked, turning to face Kyle and Ashley. "Maybe a movie or something?"

"The only thing going on anywhere tonight is Steve's party," Ashley said slowly, as if Evan were dumb. "Why wouldn't we go there?"

She probably was a very nice person, but right now she sounded like the typical cheerleader that I'd done my best to avoid for the majority of my high school life. I forced my muscles to relax.

"I don't really feel comfortable—"

"Since when has that ever stopped you from doing something?" Kyle interrupted, waving his hands around. "You're Evan Drake. Fuck them."

"It's *his* house, Kyle."

"Did he ever un-invite you outright?"

"He doesn't say much of anything to me at all, which is another reason why I shouldn't go to the party."

"You can't say that you were uninvited if he hasn't said anything to you. The invitation is still on the table, and he hasn't said otherwise." Kyle held his hands out to his sides as if to say he was a genius. "You are still invited."

"What are they going to think if Anna isn't there?" He turned back to me. "They're going to think that they won."

"We'll know the truth." I smiled shakily at him. "That's what makes the difference."

"Yeah, it's not like you're going to jump on Brittany and start humping her the minute you walk in. Right?" Kyle said, shrugging nonchalantly.

Evan slowly turned on his heel to face Kyle. Ashley slapped her boyfriend on the back of his head, and I giggled at the perplexed look on his face. Kyle fidgeted when Evan kept staring at him.

"Right. So . . . no problems." He laughed nervously, grabbing Ashley's arm and pulling her in front of him in a sad attempt to hide.

Evan turned back to me.

"You're really okay with this?"

Fourteen

Fuck no. I'm freaking out. My heart is beating ninety miles a second, and I'm terrified that you'll realize how much you miss everyone else and everything will go back to the way it was before.

"I'm really okay with this," I said instead, smiling brightly at him.

"I'll call you first thing tomorrow morning." He leaned in close to me.

"As you should."

He smiled, and I sucked in a deep breath before he kissed me.

"And you said the two of *us* were bad?" Ashley teased.

"Go away, Ashley," Evan said, pulling back from me and brushing the end of his nose against mine.

"If I remember correctly, you said it first," I stated, turning again and pointing at them.

I made the mistake of looking down the hallway and found that everyone still lingering and waiting for the warning bell had been watching us. It was easy to pick out Brittany Feldman with her jaw on the floor and her face turning a brilliant shade of red. It was almost impossible to miss her. Kyle turned to see what I was staring at and threw his hands in the air. "Move along! Mind your business, please and *thank-you*."

He turned back to us. "Sheesh."

I looked down at my feet again, tapping my fingers against my books. Weird that Kyle would choose to help me out now when before, he was happy to ignore me. I knew he was Evan's best friend, but I also knew that it didn't automatically make him mine. Was he being genuinely nice to me in an effort to make up for everything or was he just showing off for Evan, intent to run back to Steve and tell him all that was being said? I was so confused.

"This is bullshit," Evan mumbled.

"I'm sorry," I said nervously, trying to take a step away from him.

"What did I tell you about that shit?" he demanded, pulling me completely against him.

I looked up at him, my arms tightening around my books.

"You had a good . . . *life* before me."

"Anna, he was an ass," Ashley said bluntly. "Sorry, Evan, but it's true." She waved a hand in his direction, and he grunted at her. "And while he's still an ass, at least I can tolerate him a little better."

"Thanks, Ashley," he said dryly.

"Deny it; I dare you." He glared at her, and she smiled smugly when he remained silent. "That's what I thought."

"How do you put up with her?" he asked, looking at Kyle.

Kyle merely wiggled his eyebrows, and I laughed.

"Stop apologizing," he said, seeming to remember where we'd left off before Ashley had interrupted. "I'd do . . . well, I wouldn't . . . hell." He moved, and pressed his lips into a thin line. "This is what I want, right here." He squeezed me. "So stop."

The bell rang and Evan groaned.

"See you at lunch!" Kyle exclaimed.

"Huh?"

"Didn't you hear?" Ashley said, sliding her hand into Kyle's. "We're sitting with you from now on."

She shook her hair over her shoulder, waved, and towed Kyle down the hallway.

"Why are they going to be sitting with us from now on?" I asked, pointing over my shoulder at their retreating backs.

"I think this is their way of saying that they're on our side."

I sighed heavily. "I don't understand."

"You know how Christina and Vince were the only two you could talk to before I showed up?"

"Yeah."

"Kyle and Ashley are my closest friends, and they're supporting me." He grabbed my hand and kissed the back of it. "They're supporting us."

"But they . . ." I trailed off and blew out a breath. "It's going to be one of *those* days isn't it?"

"Clarify, please."

"The ones that make no sense whatsoever."

"Yes," he said. He grabbed my books from me and grinned when I stared at him in confusion.

"Come on, milady," he said in a horrible British accent. "Human physiology awaits."

I slid my hand into the crook of his arm when he offered it to me.

"You've lost your damn mind."

"Nah. You helped me find it." He leaned over and kissed me. "Thank you."

"Cheesy." I nudged him.

"Complaining?"

I grinned up at him. "No."

"Okay then."

~*~

"I'll call you as soon as I'm up and about tomorrow," he said against my lips, his hands pressed against the window of my car as he leaned in. "Are you allowed to use the phone?"

"He'll be gone all day anyway." I tilted my head. "So, you know, if you just happen to drop by . . ."

"I'm not crossing Mister Lawyer Man," he joked, cupping my cheek. "Sorry."

I sighed dramatically, and he chuckled, leaning down and kissing me again.

"Have fun, okay?"

"It's all Kyle's fault, you know," he grumbled, resting his forehead against mine. "Maybe Ashley's too."

"You had planned to go before . . ."

"Before I started hanging out with you," he said. "Everything's different now."

"Is that bad?"

"Do you really need me to answer that?"

I did everything I could to keep the smile off my face. He caught it, of course, and kissed me again.

"You should get home." He nudged his nose against mine. "I don't want you to get into any more trouble because of me."

"He's just grouchy," I said, hesitantly placing my hands on his chest.

I could feel his heartbeat as I moved my hand over it, marveling over the way it was racing much like mine always did with him around. I looked up when he covered my hand, and smiled slowly as he threaded our fingers together.

"Grouchy or not, I still want to take you on that second date. Preferably before we graduate."

"You and your expectations."

"I know. Pain right in the ass, huh?"

"You really are."

He laughed and kissed me again before stepping back from me. I sighed and let him fully link our hands together.

"Have fun tonight, okay?"

And come back to me.

"I'll try. Won't be much fun without you."

"Kiss ass."

"But, oh so true." He pulled me against him, placing one more kiss on my lips. "Talk to you tomorrow."

"Talk to you tomorrow," I said and squeezed his hand before I made myself let go and watched as he walked to his car. We were the only two left in the parking lot, everyone else damn near flying out the minute the last bell rang in anticipation of the two days of freedom we'd all been granted. It had been a normal day for me; the stares and whispers were only a little worse than usual, but not altogether something I wasn't used to. Evan had seemed tense and uptight most of the day, but he still held my hand whenever we met up in the hallway, so things couldn't have been *that* bad, right?

I sighed and finally climbed into my car, strapping the seat belt across my lap and turning the key. He waved at me when he drove past, and I waved back and then shoved the car into gear and pulled out of the parking space.

I made it home within ten minutes, very unhappy when I saw my father's truck sitting in our driveway.

Normally it wouldn't have bothered me that he was home early. Today, all I could think was that he wanted to check up on me, which really only served to annoy me. I slammed the door to my car, threw my book bag over my shoulder, stomped up the steps, and pushed through the front door.

"Anna, we need to talk," he said as soon as the front door shut behind me.

I resisted the urge to yell at him and dropped my bag to the floor before trudging my way into the living room. Surprisingly, the television was off, and he was sitting in the armchair as opposed to the couch where he usually sat. I hung my head, accepted the fact that I was about to get one hell of a lecture, and plopped myself down on the middle of the couch. After taking off my shoes and propping my feet up on the coffee table, I crossed my arms over my chest and waited for it to begin.

"You were right about some of the things you said last night, Anna, but that doesn't mean that you had a right to say them."

I narrowed my eyes at the silent television and hunched my shoulders.

"Your mom's death was really hard on me . . ."

"It hasn't been hard on me? It's not like this didn't affect me, too."

"Would you let me finish?" I grunted. "I don't know how to raise a teenage girl, Anna, and you're a complete mystery to me. I don't know what to do or what to say, so I just thought that it was better not to say anything at all. That was wrong."

I snorted.

"But this is my house, and you have to respect my rules."

"When have I ever *not* respected your rules, Dad? It's not like we were having sex in the middle of the living room when you walked in or anything!"

"Close enough."

"Right," I looked over at the front door.

"I still don't want you to be alone with him."

I ground my teeth together and said, "Fine."

"And if you're really going to date him, I want you on birth control."

He fidgeted, looking around the room like it was the first time he'd ever set foot in his own home, and I felt just as uncomfortable about where this conversation was going as he seemed to.

"I'm already on it, Dad."

"What?"

"One of the things Mom did before she got sick was take me to get them. And I know all about the birds and the bees, so please, spare me that lecture." I picked at my nails. "Was there anything else?"

"Have you been . . ."—he cleared his throat again—"have you *been* with him?"

"Oh, God." I moaned and slapped my forehead.

"Have you?"

"No, I haven't *been* with anyone."

He was quiet for a few moments, and I just kept wondering if there was any way that this could possibly get more embarrassing and aggravating.

"Are you on drugs, Anna?"

Yes, apparently it could get more embarrassing and aggravating. I had no idea where that question came from because I didn't think that I'd ever given him a reason to think that I was on drugs to begin with. If this question was because he'd seen me kiss Evan, I didn't even want to think about the other questions that he might have had in store for me.

I blinked at him, my mouth moving without sound before I finally managed to say, "Excuse me?"

"I just wanted to make sure."

"You think that little of me?"

"Of course not! I just—"

"No, Dad, I'm not on drugs. I don't smoke, I've never gone over the speed limit, I've never been suspended from school, and I've been accepted into my first choice college."

"You were?"

I wasn't sure whether I wanted to cry, scream, or throw things to get out my frustration. I'd purposely left the acceptance letter from NYU that I received a few months ago on the kitchen table so that maybe he'd see it and *say something* or at least look at it and know that his daughter was moving away from this place when she graduated. I'd even foolishly hoped that he'd be proud of me.

"Yes, I was," I said, folding my hands in my lap.

"Where's that?"

"NYU."

"You are *not* going to the city."

"I'm not going to the community college."

"Well you're not going to New York, either."

"Why not?"

"It's too far away."

"It's three hours."

"It's too far away," he said again.

"That's the point!" I exclaimed.

"You want to get away from everyone here—including me—that badly?"

"Yes," I said.

We sat in silence for what felt like forever, and I'd memorized every little groove of my fingernails before he cleared his throat.

"Well, I can't stop you."

"Do you even *want* to?"

"What is that supposed to mean?"

"I'm invisible to you, Dad; we both know it." I threw my hands in the air before letting them plop back on my thighs. "When I leave for college, what's going to change for you?"

"Anna, you're not invisible to me . . ."

"Sure I'm not, Dad." I stood and smoothed my hands over my shirt. "Does my being grounded bar running as well?"

"An hour. If you're not back within that time, I'm coming to look for you," he said, his voice detached as he stared down at the coffee table. "Because I definitely deserve to be treated like a prisoner, don't I?"

I ran up the stairs without waiting for an answer, fighting off angry tears as I changed and threw my hair up into a ponytail. I slid my sneakers on and ran back down the stairs, grabbing my iPod from the table and walking onto the porch. As I stuck the ear buds into my ears, I let out a shaky breath and bolted down the porch steps.

It didn't matter that I'd run five miles the day before and my legs had been protesting all day; I needed to get out and not be around anyone. I needed time to myself, and this was the only way I was going to get it with my dad being home.

I did my best not to think about anything but jogging my usual route and concentrating on the music flowing through the buds to my ears—nothing but the feel of the pavement underneath my feet. The wind hitting my face, and the relaxation I could only feel out here helped me to relax.

I came to the street before Steve Forrester's house—like usual—and hesitated as I reached the corner. No one would be there yet; it was doubtful that even Steve would be there yet. After all, he had to drive into Albany to beg his brother to buy some beer from the liquor store he worked at so that everyone had something to drink. I pulled my iPod out from my pocket and looked at the time. Estimating I had about five extra minutes of freedom, I started down the street.

Mr. and Mrs. Forrester were upper-class business owners that put entirely too much faith in their youngest son. They owned a successful construction company and often went into the city on the weekends to visit family for some reason or another, leaving him full reign over the white, two-story house in the middle of town. I was absolutely amazed that word had never gotten back to them about the chaos that surrounded this house whenever they weren't around, but figured that his laid-back uncle—a cop —was able to keep it under wraps for him.

I slowed down as I got to his house, noticing that his old Buick—the one his brother had beat to shit before handing it down to Steve when he got a brand new one courtesy of Mommy and Daddy Forrester—was still sitting in the driveway with a FOR SALE sign in the window.

I turned around and started back in the direction of my house, breathed in the fresh air, and tried to relax.

Chapter Ten

I slowly opened my eyes the next morning and looked around my bedroom, almost afraid that if I moved too much, something would shift and my world would come crashing down around me. I didn't sleep very well last night, every single scenario running through my mind and making me crazy to the point where I'd actually started talking to myself and thinking that I should've taken Kyle up on his offer to sneak me out of the house.

He needed an excuse to use the ski mask, after all. It would've been perfect for sneaking me out. Dad never would've known the difference, and I might have been able to get some damn sleep.

I rubbed my face before throwing the covers off and sitting up. I listened for any movement in the house and was thankful when I didn't hear anything.

When I had returned from my run, my dad was back in his spot on the couch, the remote in his hand, and his eyes glued to the documentary he'd chosen to watch. I'd rolled my eyes and went upstairs to take a shower and finish my homework.

I hadn't gotten very far on the homework bit because as soon as I saw my human physiology textbook, I thought of Evan. When I thought of Evan, I thought of him going to the party. When I thought of him going to the party, I imagined him calling me the next morning and telling me that he'd changed his mind. And that really didn't leave me in the mood to do anything but stare out my window and pray that the universe held some sort of pity for me and *would not* let that happen.

I stood, stretched, and made my way to my bedroom door, pulling it open and walking down the stairs. I went into the kitchen and a grin broke out on my face when I saw the white orchid sitting on the table. I squealed to myself and practically danced over to it, picking it up, and pressing it against my nose. I looked down to see that a disc was underneath it and picked it up. Nothing was written on the front, and I shrugged, the orchid still up to my nose as I started back up to my room with the disc in my hand.

Maybe Evan dropped it off before Dad went golfing. Maybe he dropped it off last night before he went to the party—I wasn't that far from Steve's house.

I walked into my bedroom and turned on my computer. As I waited for it to boot up, I plopped down into the seat and placed the orchid on the little space of desk in front of the monitor. When everything finally loaded, I all but ripped the DVD out of the case and stuck it into the computer, impatiently tapping my foot as it hummed at me. I opened the file and grinned at the name—*For Anna.*

That was when I got the same feeling I had last Friday when I walked in to school and found my locker vandalized, but ignored it and leaned back in the chair.

My heart raced as the computer screen went black. I placed my hands in my lap, sucking in a deep breath when I saw the back of Steve's house appear on the screen. My hands curled into fists, my nails biting into my skin as the person behind the camera wordlessly walked to the front yard. People were scattered all around, most smoking and still drinking as they laughed like idiots. The camera zoomed in on Evan sitting in the front seat of the Buick. He was holding a blue party cup half-full of some liquid I probably didn't care to know about and smoking what looked to be a joint. My breath caught as the person behind the camera practically ran over to him.

Evan grinned lazily. "You want?" His voice slurred as he held out the joint.

When the person behind the camera didn't speak, Evan lifted his arm in a *your loss* gesture before bringing it to his lips, crossing his ankles on the ground. He wore that red and blue striped shirt he'd had on a few days ago with a pair of dark jeans and military boots.

"Evan!"

He looked up and his lazy smile returned when Steve entered the frame and leaned against the car door and poked his head through the open window.

"What are you doing out here all alone?"

"Chillin'."

"Cool . . . cool. So, tell me about Arianna Weller, dude."

I tightened my hands into fists, not caring that I might end up drawing my own blood if I kept it up.

"Arianna Weller," Evan said slowly, smoke fuming from his mouth. "She's not very attractive, is she, Steve?"

I choked and placed one hand flat on my chest, staring at the screen.

"Possibly one of the most unattractive girls in our entire school." He slid lower into the seat and stretched his legs out in front of him. "Probably never even gotten laid."

"Probably never been kissed, either," Steve piped up.

"Like the movie!" Evan laughed, the end of the joint glowing in the darkness of the car. "Although, even Drew Barrymore is hotter than Arianna."

"Her chin annoys me."

"At least she *has* one."

"Score!" Steve shouted, leaning farther into the car and slapping Evan's arm. "You think you'll ever fuck her, Evan?"

"Nah." He sat up, his head tilted to the side. "I don't think I'll ever be that desperate—or that obliterated."

As it faded to black, every inch of me felt numb. I was gasping for breath—that much I was aware of—but everything else just became a big blur to me. All I could think was that I was right.

He'd never changed. This was all just a joke to him. *I* was just a joke to him, and I'd let it happen.

I clenched my teeth together and screamed through them, burying my hands in my hair. Then I pulled, not feeling the pain I so desperately needed before I pulled out the DVD. I threw it onto my desk, grabbed the orchid, and stormed down the stairs.

The garbage disposal worked on and off most of the time, and I usually found it easier to throw things in the garbage can than to deal with the aftermath of picking out leftovers from the drain, but right now, I wanted this cut into pieces. Whether I was his social experiment and all of this was a great hoax designed to humiliate me and make him seem more superior to all of his friends or this was some elaborate plan to break up with me, I didn't know.

I no longer cared.

I shoved the orchid down the drain and reached over to flip on the switch, watching as it disappeared. My breath was still shuddering, and I was vaguely aware of the tears that were rolling down my cheeks as I stared at the drain, but I couldn't bring myself to care. I flipped off the switch and wiped my cheeks, and I made a sound I couldn't define as I started back toward the stairs.

I was such an *idiot* to think that he could ever change; to think that anything he'd ever said to me meant anything. Was everything we'd been through leading to this moment where I was beyond hurt or embarrassed, past anything any of them had ever done to me before?

I stopped at the bottom of the stairs and looked up at them, my vision going blurry as tears filled my eyes again. Gripping the rail, I started up the stairs, breathing heavily.

He hadn't completely gained my trust, but he'd been damn close, and that's what pissed me off and hurt the most. I'd let my guard down more than I normally would have with anyone other than Christina and Vince. And this is what I got for thinking that anyone else was worth any of my time and energy; for giving someone a second chance.

When the phone rang, I clenched my jaw. Wiping my face off one more time before I made my way over to the phone, I snatched it up, cleared my throat, and put it to my ear.

"Hello?"

"Good morning, girlfriend."

My eyes narrowed and tears fell.

"You don't need to call me that anymore, Evan," I said coolly, clenching my hand into a fist and staring down at the floor. "I got your gifts this morning, and everything is loud and fucking clear."

"What?" he asked, confused. "What are you talking about?"

"Don't play stupid with me, Evan! How *dare* you call me after that? How *dare* you say any of that? You . . . you're . . . I'm a human being, Evan, and you can't just treat me this way!"

I was shrieking at this point and only realized it when I stopped talking and the silence rang heavily in my ears. My heartbeat was erratic, and I could feel every inch of me shaking as tears continued to drip off my chin.

"Please tell me what you're talking about, Anna."

"Stop it! You know exactly what I'm talking about! I don't know why you couldn't just say it to my face and break up with me that way! There was no need for this! I didn't . . . I've never . . ."

My legs gave out beneath me, and I dropped to the floor hard, realizing too late that I was a sobbing mess, and he knew it. It only served to piss me off, but I couldn't catch my breath, and I couldn't do anything but clutch the phone to my ear and want to kill him.

"Anna, please," he begged, almost sounding sincere. "Please tell me what I did."

"You *know* what you did."

"No, I don't! Please, just *talk* to me."

"How much did you drink last night, Evan, that you wouldn't remember calling me the most unattractive girl you've ever seen? Or saying that you'd never sleep with me because you'd never be that desperate or obliterated?"

"What are you . . . ? Oh, no," he whispered. "No, Anna, no, no, no, you don't—"

"Fuck you," I whispered, angrily wiping my face. "I'm *done*."

"Anna, listen to me!"

I slammed the phone back on the cradle and stood up, trying my hardest to catch my breath as I ran my hands through my hair and started back toward the stairs. The phone rang again, but I ignored it, keeping my eyes front and center as I climbed the stairs.

What I'd feared about last night had come true, and it was no one's fault but my own. I'd let him in, and all it did was get me hurt and make me more of a laughing stock around the school than I'd ever been. I'd let myself almost forget how cruel and heartless he could be when he put his mind to it, and that was my mistake. I'd forgotten that he could be an asshole, and I ended up hurting because of it.

I made it back to my bedroom, slowly closing the door behind me and leaning against it. Everything was the same as it had been two weeks ago; I was alone, and there were only a few more months until graduation. I had no one to leave behind who would miss me that much, and nothing but passing my classes and getting the *hell* out of this town mattered.

With a shaky breath, I wiped away the tears from my cheeks for the last time that day before walking over to my dresser and grabbing an old pair of sweatpants and a t-shirt.

Evan Drake was no longer worth anything to me, much less my tears.

Fourteen

~*~

I looked up when I thought I heard footsteps making their way toward me, and I ripped my ear buds out, holding my soapy hands out in front of me.

"No!" I exclaimed. "The floor's wet, and your boots are dirty!"

My dad looked down at me, his eyebrows raised and his mouth parted in something I was assuming was shock.

I was on my hands and knees in the kitchen, scrubbing the hell out of the floor because working on homework hadn't done anything but make everything worse. The cycle that had started last night when I had tried to concentrate on the human physiology paper only worsened, and I'd come downstairs to get a drink.

I noticed that the floor was filthy—along with the rest of the house—and had abandoned my homework to clean it. The phone hadn't stopped ringing, and I'd eventually grabbed my iPod to drown out the annoying sound. I didn't check the answering machine for fear that I wouldn't be strong enough to not listen to the messages that may or may not have been there.

"Uh, Anna . . . what are you doing?"

"I'm cleaning. What does it look like I'm doing?" I snapped.

"Why?" he asked slowly.

"Well, if you haven't noticed, the floor was dirty, and it needed to be cleaned. I'm going to vacuum the living room when I'm done here so I hope that you don't have any shows you want to watch."

"Anna, it's Saturday."

"I don't know the stupid schedules!"

"No, that's not . . . why are you cleaning the floor on a Saturday afternoon?"

"I'm grounded," I snapped again. "What else would you propose I do?"

"Well . . . watch television?"

"Like there's anything I'd be interested in."

"Well then, how about you go talk to Evan?"

My eyes narrowed, and my heart thumped painfully in my chest.

"Why would I do that?" I asked through my teeth.

"Because he says he's been standing outside for the past three hours."

My eyes stung, and I grabbed my ear buds again, sticking them back in my ears and falling forward on my hands. "He can stand out there all night if he wants. I thought I wasn't supposed to be alone with him anyway."

"Well . . . you're not technically alone with him so . . ." I jumped when he tugged an ear bud out, and I glared at him as he squatted on my *clean* floor with his *dirty* boots as I'd *specifically* asked him not to do. "He doesn't look so hot."

"I don't *care*."

"Want to tell me what's going on?"

"Nothing's going on," I spat. "And nothing will ever be going on ever again. He can stand out there until bright and early Monday morning; I don't care."

"You were angry because I wouldn't let you be alone with him, and now that I'm allowing it, you want nothing to do with him?"

"Yes."

"Is this some teenage rebellion thing?"

"No, Dad, it's not. Evan and I are over. Plain and fucking simple."

"Watch your mouth."

"Get off my floor."

"Go talk to Evan."

"Why does it matter to you now? You wouldn't listen to me the other day, and now you won't leave me the hell alone when it comes to him? Would you make up your mind, *please*?"

"Did you get the flower and the disc?"

I glared at him again, the edges of my vision tinted red.

"Yes," I said through my teeth. "Where'd you find them?"

"On the front step this morning when I left. Was it from him?"

"I'm not sure." I stuck my nose in the air and grabbed the sponge from where I'd left it. "It doesn't matter."

"You really think so?"

"Yes, I really do."

"I hope you can live with regrets, then."

"I've got plenty of regrets, Dad," I said, furiously rubbing at a scuffmark that had been imbedded into the floor for as long as I'd been alive.

"You're willing to add another one to that list then?"

"Why should it matter?"

"My greatest regret was not telling your mother more often how much I loved her. We'd gotten into a pretty big fight that night. That's why she was out driving around so late. Couldn't stand the sight of me, she'd said." I looked up at him, my jaw aching from how hard I had my teeth clenched together.

"I never thought that those words would be the last I'd ever say to her. I can't change that now, but maybe if I'd just . . ." He sighed, and my heart broke a little more. I didn't know that he'd been holding on to this guilt for so long.

"We were fighting over my golf clubs. It was such a foolish, trivial thing. She just wanted me to put them in the closet. I didn't know what the big deal was. I could've prevented her from leaving the house that night if I'd only put them away like she'd asked."

"Dad, this is nothing like that."

"I met your mother in high school, and she was one of the two best things that had ever happened to me. You were the other." He nodded toward the windows facing the front yard. "Go talk to him. The floor won't go anywhere."

I'd managed to briefly forget what had sparked this conversation in the first place, but felt the anger flare up once more when Evan was mentioned.

"Why are you pushing this so damn hard? Why are you suddenly giving me advice that I don't want?"

"I'm your dad. That's what I'm here for, isn't it?" I snorted, and he rolled his eyes. "I'm trying, Anna."

"Everyone's *trying*, but no one can actually just *do* what they said they're going to. No one can just . . . *not* torture me and hurt me. No, the best I can ever get is *trying*."

"It's better than nothing, isn't it?"

"At this point, no!" I exclaimed, throwing the sponge into the bucket of water as I sat back on my heels. "I've settled for the crappy end of the stick my entire life, and the one time I might *finally* be happy with something I didn't think I'd ever get, it gets ripped away because *he's* an asshole. So no, Dad, I don't think *trying* is good enough anymore."

"I'm sorry that your life has been so terrible for you," he said dryly, standing and brushing his hands on his jeans. "Let me know when you need me to sign the loan papers for your school, all right? Maybe I can do that right, huh?"

I screamed in frustration and hopped up from the floor, ripping my ear buds out of my ears and yanking my iPod from my pocket. I threw it haphazardly onto the table by the door and ran up the stairs, scrubbing my eyes as I made it into my bedroom. I grabbed the disc still sitting on my computer desk and slapped it back into the case before I ran back down the stairs, swallowing the hiccups and tears that were building in my throat.

"Where are you going?" my dad demanded.

"I'm going to talk to him, Dad!" I yelled, hating the way my voice was shaking. "Since you seem to think he's the second coming of Christ and all!"

"Very funny, Anna."

I pulled open the door and stalked out onto the porch as Evan scrambled up from his seated position on the driveway in front of his car. I sniffled against my better judgment as I made my way down the steps and stopped at the bottom. The anger I'd felt a second ago disappeared and was replaced with defeat and acceptance.

"Anna, listen to me—"

"I have absolutely no desire to hear anything you have to say," I interrupted, walking down the steps to meet him. "I don't care what you want because it no longer matters to me."

"You're not—"

"I don't care anymore, Evan. You've made your point, and your social experiment is over."

"Anna, it's not like that!" he exclaimed. "That wasn't me!"

"Yes, it was." I laughed sarcastically. "Unless you have a long-lost twin brother, I'm pretty positive that was you."

"Please, let me explain!"

"No." I placed the case against his chest and nearly flinched when he trapped my hand with his. "We're stuck together for human physiology, but I'm done with you when it comes to everything else."

"You're not giving me a chance."

"I *gave* you a chance, and this is what I got for it. I'm done. Get off my property."

"Anna, please listen to me!"

"Leave me *alone*."

I slid my hand out and turned back to the house. I felt a suspicious ache in my chest as I climbed the stairs.

"I'm sorry!" he yelled. "Anna, I'm sorry!"

"So am I! Now leave."

I slipped back into the house and sucked in a shaky breath, closing my eyes.

"That's not quite what I was talking about," my dad insisted from the kitchen.

"Get off my floor," I said, opening my eyes and walking back into the kitchen. "I have work to do."

"Whatever he did," he said, leaning over and pulling back the lace curtains on the kitchen windows. "He wants to make it right."

"Shut *up*, Dad."

"Just look, Anna."

"Will you get off my floor then?"

"I'll even leave the house if you want me to."

I stalked to his side, yanking the curtain from him and looking out. My face fell as I saw Evan hunched over the steering wheel in his car, his hands clasped tightly on the dashboard in front of him.

"Doesn't matter," I said, silently cursing when my voice cracked. "I'm done with him."

I turned away from the window, pressing my lips together as I sank back to my knees, rolled up my sleeves, and stuck my hand back into the soapy bucket.

"All right," he finally said, and I heard him walk around me. "Why are there eighteen messages on the machine?"

I didn't want to think about the messages and voicemails on my cell phone. Fortunately, I didn't even know where it was or if it was charged.

"I don't care and don't you *dare* listen to them when I'm within hearing distance."

"You can't avoid him forever."

"Why the sudden interest in my life, Dad?" I asked, sitting back on my heels. "Why now?"

"There's always been an interest, but relationships are something that I can help you with. You should listen to what he has to say."

"I already know what he's going to say."

"You can read minds now? I wasn't aware."

I glared at him.

"I thought you said that you'd leave," I said through my teeth.

He held his hands up at his sides, palms facing me.

"I'm going, I'm going."

"Mm-hm." I dropped back to my hands and searched for the sponge in the bucket. "I won't be going anywhere."

"If he's still out there when I get back, I'm inviting him inside."

I looked up at him through a curtain of hair as I slapped the sponge on the floor with a wet smack.

"You do that," I said, my voice low.

"I mean it. If you feel anything for him—"

"I feel *nothing* for him."

"I don't believe that."

"Why not?"

"You don't get on your hands and knees to scrub floors, Anna. You use the mop and you do it maybe once a month when you think of it."

"Well, maybe if you—"

"I'm not complaining!" he exclaimed. "I'm happy that you think of it at all. I'm just pointing out that it's not something that you do on a regular basis."

"*Why* are you pointing it out?"

"Because you say you don't feel anything for him, but you're not facing whatever happened."

"I'm not . . . go already," I demanded, motioning toward the door. "I don't want to talk about this anymore."

"You'll have to face it sooner rather than later."

"Well, I don't have to do it right now, do I?" I began scrubbing at the scuffmark again. "I'm sure I'll be done by the time you get home."

"Think about it, Anna."

I grunted and listened as he finally walked out of the house. I heard him speaking to Evan and ground my teeth together, furiously scrubbing at the mark on the floor.

Why wouldn't it come out already?

I listened carefully for the door on his truck close, listened even harder when he pulled out of the driveway and drove off. I looked down at the scuffmark I'd been agonizing over for the majority of the day and leaned back on my heels again. I looked around at the half-cleaned floor and grabbed the sponge, once again throwing it into the bucket before I grabbed the handle and stood up. I cleaned up the rest of my bright idea, freezing when I heard footsteps on the porch. I ran up the stairs and into my room. I threw my dirty clothes off before diving into my bed in just my underwear and bra, pulling my pillow over my head and willing sleep to come.

I didn't want to deal with anything anymore.

Chapter Eleven

He was on my doorstep Sunday morning, and I made my dad answer it when he knocked. I hid like a coward at the top of the stairs, listening to their mixed voices, but not really hearing a word as I sat ready to bolt into my room if my dad let him in.

I couldn't deal with Evan just yet. I was working myself up to Monday morning, and for the life of me, I failed to understand why he was trying so hard, unless his plans had been ruined and he had more in store. None of it made any sense, and I hated the way he seemed to be so intent on making any of this right.

The other part that was confusing was that he'd alienated all of his friends—at least, I thought he had. Maybe that was all part of the joke, too. They had to make it look as authentic as possible so that I'd actually believe all his crap to begin with.

Ugh, I was so *stupid*. I should've known better—I'd been around them my entire life. Why I thought Evan Drake would be able to change because of things that *I* said and did was laughable, and I should've known something wasn't right. *I should've known.*

I snapped back to the present when I heard the front door close, tensing and listening carefully for an extra set of footsteps.

"Anna, he's gone!" my dad yelled up to me.

"Really?"

"I promise you that he's gone."

I got up, smoothing down my shirt as I walked down the stairs, stopping when my dad stepped in front of me. He thrust a white envelope in front of my face, my name written on it in Evan's undeniably neat handwriting.

"Throw it out," I said, my voice low as I stared at the way he'd curled the end of the *A*.

"Open it."

"I mean it."

"So do I," my dad said easily.

"I have no reason to—"

"You didn't see him, Anna. I don't think he's slept."

"Good."

"You don't mean that."

"He's caused me plenty of sleepless nights. He owes me a few," I spat bitterly.

"You're being immature."

"I'm eighteen; I'm supposed to be."

"You've never been like this before."

"Things change. People change."

He merely raised an eyebrow at me, and I glared at him. I hadn't told him anything about what had happened, and I was surprised that he'd seemed to catch on. For a man who hadn't taken notice of what was going on in my life, he sure seemed to know a lot.

He shook the envelope in my face again, and I snatched it out of his hand, stalking into the kitchen. I had it held over the trashcan, staring down at the remains of our breakfast as I fingered the edges.

"I don't know what you feel for him, Anna," my dad said from the doorway of the kitchen, "but it's obviously the same thing he feels for you. Open it."

"I can't." My voice cracked and I closed my eyes. "Whatever is in this will *not* make what he said all right."

"It might not," he agreed. "There are two things that can happen here: either that will explain everything or it'll explain nothing. You're too young for so many regrets, and if I know you like I think I do, throwing that envelope away and not knowing what may or may not be in there will follow you around and drive you crazy."

"Dad, you don't—"

"I know the way he looked when I opened the door. I know the way you looked when you woke up this morning. Neither of you is very excited about this new development."

"He could be putting on an act, Dad! Don't you *get* that?" I exclaimed, turning to face him and pointing at him with the envelope. "He could be pretending because he just wants to hurt me some more!"

"That's not what I saw this morning, Anna. I saw something very close to heartbreak on his face, and if he can feel that way over losing my daughter, I have to give him some respect because he *knows* what he's lost!"

"I can't do this," I said, walking over to him. "I have homework to do."

"All right." He moved out of my way.

I stomped back up the stairs and into my room, throwing the envelope down on my computer desk as if it had bitten me. I placed my hands over my throat, stared at the envelope until I couldn't take it anymore, and turned away.

Not right now.

~*~

I waited until the last possible second to go inside the school. I'd sat in my car in the farthest corner of the parking lot, watching everyone walk inside, chatting, laughing, and completely unafraid to pass through the double doors. I kept my head down when I made it inside, my stomach in knots, feeling like I was going to spontaneously combust at any moment as I shoved my things into my locker. I grabbed my human physiology book and made it into the classroom as the second bell rang, my eyes trained on the floor as I made it over to my table. Evan was already there, and I could feel his eyes on me as I sat down. Looking straight ahead, I noticed that Steve's head wasn't in my way as it usually was. I felt a small sense of relief that I wouldn't have to deal with him today as well.

"Anna," Evan whispered when everyone was seated and Mr. Streeter had started roll call.

I ignored him, grinding my teeth as I grabbed my pen and played with it nervously. I managed to call out a shaky *here* when my name was called before tapping the end of the pen against my notebook and wiggling in my seat.

"Did you see them?" he said, when I didn't say anything.

I shifted uncomfortably, trying to concentrate on anything but what he was saying.

"Anna, *please*," he begged.

"See *what*? Pictures of me in some humiliating pose plastered in the hallway? No, I didn't," I snapped in a whisper, still fidgeting with my pen as Mr. Streeter finally started the lesson I wouldn't be paying attention to.

"You didn't open it."

"Open what?"

"Did your Dad give it to you? He said he would."

I closed my eyes and did my best to block him out.

That stupid envelope had been taunting me ever since my dad gave it to me. I'd tried my best not to think about it, but that hadn't worked. It didn't help seeing Evan in person, either.

"I got it," I finally whispered back.

"Why didn't you open it?"

"I had things to do."

"Anna, I'm *sorry*. You have to let me explain."

"I don't have to let you do *anything*, Evan. You won. Give it up. Whatever else you had planned, I'm sorry, but I'm not going to keep playing this game."

"There is no game and I didn't win. There was nothing to win. In fact, I'm pretty sure that I lost it all!"

"Drake! Weller!"

We both looked up to find Mr. Streeter staring at us along with the rest of the class.

Huh. Guess we raised our voices a bit.

"Sorry," Evan mumbled, hunching his shoulders.

I said my apologies as well and flipped open my notebook, the pen still held tightly in my hand as I tried to focus on the words the teacher had written on the blackboard.

The rest of the class passed without incident until Mr. Streeter gave us ten minutes before the bell rang as free time, reminding us that the science fair was this Saturday.

"Will you come over tonight?" he asked, his eyes trained on the books piled in front of him. "We need to get everything for our project worked out."

He was right and I hated it. We still had a lot of work to do and barely any time to do it.

"I'll call my dad during lunch," I said.

"Thanks." He played with the edges of his notebook.

"Will you ever talk to me again?" he whispered.

I almost faltered, the tone of his voice nearly breaking my heart, but I sucked in a deep breath, staring hard down at my books. "I'm talking to you now."

"About anything else but the project?"

I shrugged, rubbing my thumb on the binding of my textbook. "I don't know."

"Please just let me—"

"No, Evan."

"Anna, please—"

"Stop it," I whispered, my eyes watering as I committed the doodles on the cover of my book to memory.

"That was from a party about three weeks ago—"

"Stop it, Evan."

"I didn't know you then, Anna. It doesn't make it right, but—"

"Evan, *stop*."

Thankfully, the bell rang, and I think I was the first one up and out of my chair, practically running to the door and not caring whom I knocked over on my way there.

I should've stayed home.

~*~

I pulled up behind Evan as he parked in his driveway and placed my hands in my lap.

It had been one hell of a confusing day, and I just wanted it over with. No one had said a word to me today—aside from Vince and Christina who had told me that they'd left the party almost as soon as they'd arrived—when I'd finally showed up in the cafeteria after calling my father who agreed to let me go because he was all about Evan these days.

I had never gone through a school day where no one had made any kind of comment to me, and I wasn't entirely sure what to do about it. There was a lot of staring and a few snickers that only made me speed up my pace as I walked by. I'd managed to avoid Kyle and Ashley, not entirely sure if they'd want to talk to me anyway but wanting to cover all of my bases while I could.

I was mentally exhausted, and the last thing I really wanted to do was sit in Evan's house with him as we worked on this stupid science fair project that started this whole damn mess.

A few more months, Anna, and you're gone. You won't see him, and you won't have to deal with any more of this crap. You can start over and things will be better. You'll make *them better.*

I grabbed my bag and pushed open the door. I got out and met him at the front of my car, and he offered me a weak smile before walking toward the house. I followed behind him, and he held the door open for me. He took off his shoes and hung his keys on a rack by the door. Figuring it was okay, I took off my shoes as well and checked to see if my socks were clean.

"We can work in the dining room," he said.

"Okay." I hitched my bag up higher on my shoulder as he walked ahead of me and into the living room.

"Evan? Is that you?"

"Yeah, Mom," he called, nervously rubbing the back of his neck. "We're here."

"We?"

She popped out of some doorway, and I stuffed one hand in my pocket, hooking the other around the strap of my bag. Did she know what happened? Did she know anything about how her son had treated me all these years? Did she think it was justified?

"Oh, Anna," she exclaimed, grinning and walking over to me, hugged me and kissed both of my cheeks before stepping back. "Are you staying for dinner?"

"My dad actually wants me home by six," I lied, trying to offer her a smile. "He's got to eat, too."

"Oh," she said, pouting and then smiling reassuringly. "Well, all right, then. Make yourself at home. If either of you need me for anything, I'll be in my office."

"Thanks, Mom."

She walked by Evan and squeezed his shoulder. He offered her a pathetic smile, and I wished we'd never been paired up for this stupid science fair.

After she left, we both shifted awkwardly as we stood in a silence that seemed to drag on forever.

"Did you want something to drink?" he finally asked.

"Water, I guess," I said, looking over in his general direction.

"Dining room is through there," he pointed to an archway across the room, "I'll be there in a second if you want to go sit down."

I walked through the pristine living room and through the archway, looking around the equally elegant dining room and plopping down into one of the red and gold cushioned high-back chairs. Unzipping my bag, I pulled out the folders and notebooks and placed them on the table. I searched around in the front pocket for a pen, when I felt the envelope and pulled my hand out.

I reached back in and pulled it out, running my thumbs across my name as my heart pounded in my chest. I turned it over and flipped it open, greeted with the back of what looked to be photo paper. My hands shaking, I pulled it out and dropped the envelope to the table, seeing that there was more of his handwriting on the back.

This is what I did all night, Anna.

I licked my lips and held my breath as I turned it over to find a picture of him wearing a black t-shirt, and a pair of dark blue jeans and white sneakers. He sat in a corner with a beer bottle in his hands. He was staring off in the opposite direction and seemed completely oblivious to whoever was taking the picture. The orange date stamp in the bottom corner of the picture proudly declared last Friday's date.

It didn't make sense.

I dropped that one to the table and flipped over the other one, my breath whooshing out of my lungs when I saw a very impressive picture of Evan punching Steve in the jaw; Evan's face was red and his lips were pressed into a tight line. Once again, the date stamp declared it was last Friday.

What the hell was going on?

I dropped that one to the table and flipped over the last one, my mouth dropping open when I saw him. He was standing in front of Brittany and Grace. He had one hand in the air and pointed at something with his mouth open in what I assumed was mid-yell. Stupid confusing date stamp was there, too.

I didn't understand.

I dropped that one to the table as well, leaned forward, and cradled my head in my hands. I concentrated on breathing evenly as I tried to sort out the muddled thoughts in my head.

"Ashley wants to be a photographer."

I looked up at him as he carefully set a glass of water on the table, avoiding my gaze as he eased into the chair next to me.

"She takes that damn camera with her everywhere she goes and always makes sure to document everything that happens." He looked up at me, and I dropped my hands, letting them fall into my lap. "The video you saw was not from last Friday."

I closed my eyes briefly and then opened them, snatching up the picture of him hitting Steve. I held it out to him, shaking it.

"Good shot, isn't it?"

I tilted my head. He sighed and took the picture from me, looking down at it.

"He said some things"—he set the picture aside—"about you."

I looked away, fidgeting.

"It pissed me off."

I pushed the one of him with Brittany and Grace over to him. I watched him from the corner of my eye as he rubbed the back of his neck.

"I was telling them to go fuck themselves," he said, craning his neck to look around and make sure that no one heard him, I assumed. "They agreed with what Steve said about you."

"What'd he say?"

"It's not—"

"Tell me," I demanded.

He flicked the picture away from him, rested his arms on the table, and leaned down to rest his chin on his hands.

"He said that I must like being the prettier one in the relationship and having the upper hand with you. That he wasn't sure how I was going to . . ."—he groaned—". . . how I was going to sleep with you without getting sick or being crushed."

My eyes immediately watered, and I looked away, wanting nothing more than to curl up into a ball and disappear. When my lips began to quiver, I pressed them together and closed my eyes.

"You hit him," I whispered.

"Fractured his jaw."

"You hit him for *me*."

"Yes," he said, his voice strained.

"Is he pressing charges?"

"He'd have to tell his parents about what happened while they were away. It's amazing how many people kept his parties a secret from his parents."

"How is he going to explain his jaw, then?"

"Baseball practice."

"I don't . . ."—I rubbed my eyes—"We have work to do."

"Anna, don't you . . . ?"

"I have a lot to sort out and I need time to think, so please don't talk to me about it right now." With his shoulders hunched in defeat, he looked so pitiful I almost felt bad for him.

"Okay," he said. "Can I just say one more thing?"

I leaned back in the chair and fidgeted.

"I've made a lot of mistakes when it comes to you, and I said a lot of things that were uncalled for and horrible. I thought I knew you then, and that I had a right to judge you, but I was an idiot. You didn't deserve any of that. I'm sorry, Anna."

I stared down at my hands, and then leaned forward and placed my hands on top of my books.

"Did you want to work on the paper or the board?" I asked.

"I'll work on the board," he said. "Unless you want to."

"No, that's fine. I need your part, though," I said as I hunted in my bag for a pen.

"Okay." He got up. "I left my bag in the kitchen. I'll be right back."

After he walked out, I leaned over my books, tapping my forehead against them and groaning.

At this stage of the game, I couldn't *not* believe him. The proof was sitting right in front of me. I could see that he was sorry about it, and he'd done nothing but apologize to me since. The fact of the matter, though, was that he'd still said those things. He'd been saying them since middle school and realizing that no matter what kind of person he'd recently turned in to, all of the comments and the insults from the past still hurt *now*. I couldn't just put those feelings aside when I'd been dealing with them for so long, when I'd been so bitter toward him and his friends for so long. A big part of me didn't fully understand why he was so willing to turn his back on his friends and his reputation for me.

I looked up when he walked back into the room, and I stared hard at him as he sat down again.

"What?" he asked.

"Why?" I blurted. "Why are you putting so much time and effort into me?"

"Because you're worth it," he said in a soft voice.

"This is not a L'Oreal commercial, Evan."

He slouched back into his chair, crossing his arms over his chest, and stared at the table. "I don't know what else you want me to say to you," he said. "I meant everything I've said, and you don't . . ."—he leaned forward and rested his elbows on the table to cradle his head—"I'm not that person anymore, Anna. I know that the video was only three weeks ago, but you know as well as I do; three weeks can change everything. Looking back, I didn't like the person I was, and I know right now that I'd never go back to that. I need you to trust me on that. If you don't then I don't know what else to do. I'll leave you alone when this is done, and that'll be it."

The ache I'd been feeling for the past three days got worse, and I looked down at my books again.

"Okay," I whispered.

He was quiet and out of curiosity, I looked up at him, my heart beating faster when I saw that his hands were covering his face. I was at a complete loss for words, not knowing what was going on in his head. It was then that I noticed the faint bruising on the knuckles of his right hand, and I glanced over at the pictures still littering the tabletop.

"What do you want to put on the board?" he asked, his voice strained.

"Whatever you think is best."

He stared out the windows in front of him and crossed his arms on the table, and then he leaned over, unzipped his bag, and pulled out his notebook. He flipped it open and ripped out a few sheets, handing them over to me and snapping it closed again. "I know that you don't want to be here," he said. "If you just want to do that at home, you can go."

"Are you kicking me out?"

"No. I'm just giving you a reason to leave like I know you want to. I'm trying to make this as easy as possible for you."

"You think this is easy?"

He shrugged.

"It's not . . . I feel like every part of me has just been . . . ripped open. Like everything I'm feeling or thinking is on display and I can't . . ."—I closed my eyes when they filled again—"I hate feeling that way. I hate that you made me feel that way. I hate that I let you get to me and made me forget about everything you'd ever done . . ."

"You hate me, I get it."

"I don't!" I exclaimed, opening my eyes to look at him again. "I just need to figure things out."

I stared at his profile, and his jaw twitched.

"You have no intentions of ever trusting me, do you?" he finally asked.

"I don't know what to do, Evan."

"Are you staying?"

"Unless you really want me to go."

"I don't ever want you to go," he whispered before looking away from me and opening his notebook again.

We spent the rest of the afternoon in silence, only asking questions when necessary. His mother poked her head in at one point, and he offered her that pathetically sad smile; I almost bolted out of the house, but she didn't seem upset with me at all and actually smiled at me before letting us know she was going to start dinner and disappearing. I packed up my things at quarter to six, and Evan walked me to the door.

"I'll see you tomorrow," he said as I slid back into my shoes.

"Yeah."

"Drive safe."

"Thanks."

I turned from the door and fingered my keys as I walked to my car. I made it home and sluggishly walked into the still-empty house before locking the door behind me and walking up the stairs to my room.

I still wanted to be mad at him. I wanted to feel justified being mad at him and not talking to him, but the truth was all I felt was a resounding ache. I don't think I'd ever been more confused than I was right this moment, and I didn't know what to do about it.

Chapter Twelve

"You're in my way."

I looked up from my sluggish pace and saw Adam standing in front of me, a twisted smile on his face as he stood in front of me. I stared hard at him, not in the mood for any of this crap today.

My head was everywhere but where it was supposed to be. I hadn't gotten much sleep the night before because I was too busy thinking about everything that Evan had said and trying to make sense of it all. I had somehow managed to finish the human physiology paper, although I had no idea how and even managed to have an actual conversation with my father over dinner.

Human physiology that morning had been pure torture. Evan remained silent throughout the entire class, saying a quick *good morning* when he'd first walked in before concentrating unnaturally hard on his notes.

When the bell rang, he told me that his practice Thursday that would be longer than usual because there was a game on Friday, so we wouldn't be able to get together to work on our project.

I told him that we'd have to definitely work on it tonight to get all the details down for our presentation, and he'd agreed before telling me that he'd see me later and walking out.

Part of me was relieved that he hadn't tried to talk to me more, but there was still a little part of me that felt somewhat disappointed, which aggravated me beyond reason, and I'd spent my entire economics class trying not to tear my hair out.

The entire day was one big mind screw, and I didn't like it at all. For once in my life, I'd wished that absolutely nothing had changed. I hadn't exactly enjoyed being picked on and teased by almost everyone, but at least I was used to it.

"Go around me, Adam," I said through my teeth.

"Well, I'd like to"—he tapped his chin—"but your fat ass is taking up the whole hallway."

I couldn't deal with *this* on top of everything else. Something inside of me just seemed to snap, and I couldn't control my mouth. "Do you get off on saying things like that?" I snapped, narrowing my eyes at him. "Does it make you feel good about yourself?"

"I . . ."

"Do you even realize that when you leave this school and go off to college that you won't be the badass you seem to think you are? Do you realize that you will get nowhere if you keep acting like this?"

"Listen, fat ass—"

"Yeah, go ahead and make fun of the way I look. Make yourself feel better. Just know that next year, I'll be off to NYU and you'll be flipping burgers. Get off your high horse, Adam."

With that, I shoved by him and stalked into the empty classroom, plopping down into my seat and leaning forward to cradle my head in my hands.

"You all right, Anna?"

It was Kyle. My avoidance techniques had clearly failed me today.

"Fine," I said, shifting uneasily.

"Are you sure?"

"Yeah." I stared down at my books and licked my lips nervously.

"I told you to leave her alone, Adam."

I heard Evan's voice out in the hallway, and I cringed, lacing my hands together and squeezing tightly. He was defending me against someone who used to be one of his good friends. Despite the fact that I told him I needed to think and couldn't talk to him about it while I did it, he was still willing to stand up for me and protect me. It was definitely a step in the right direction, but there was just so much going on in my head right now that trusting him was still one of the very last things I could do right now.

"You're still picking the cow over us? What the hell is wrong with you?"

"I grew up. Maybe you should do the same. Leave her alone."

Kyle and I sat in an awkward silence, and I wondered what he wanted and why he wasn't out in the hallway with Ashley like he usually was in between classes. I didn't hear Evan's voice out in the hallway anymore and breathed a small sigh of relief.

"I'm still one of the people that you want to talk to, right?" Kyle finally asked.

"Before I was with Evan, you didn't want to be seen talking to me either," I said, looking up at him before going back to my lap.

"I'm sorry about that, but it's all different now. Everything's changed."

"Nothing's changed."

"He didn't do anything all night, Anna. He sat in a corner, looking at his watch every five minutes, and every time I went over to him, all he did was ask if we were done so that he could go home."

"Kyle, I'm not—"

"Yes, he did say those things," he interrupted. "And no, it wasn't right. But a lot of shit has changed since then, and he'd take it back if he could. He *wants* to."

"He could go back to being that person—"

"If he was going to do it, he would've done it when you told him to leave you alone. Hell, he wouldn't have sat outside your house all weekend if he was going to go back to being *that* person."

"How do you know about all of this?"

"Who do you think he talked to?" Kyle chuckled, resting his elbow on my desk. "He's all torn up about it."

"He really hit Steve?"

"Why do you think Steve's been out?"

"I thought his jaw was just fractured."

"Now he's got it wired shut for the next six weeks and has to eat through a straw."

My eyes bulged, and my mouth dropped open. Kyle laughed at me, grabbed my shoulder, and shook me gently.

"He really told Brittany and Grace to fuck off?"

"That was my favorite part of the night."

"Who put it on my doorstep, Kyle?"

"Probably one of *the girls*. They're vindictive bitches, and they were pissed that Evan wasn't giving them the time of day anymore."

"Makes sense," I said, tracing the binding on my textbook. "Does Ashley hate me again?"

"She's giving you time. I'm just an impatient bastard, and neither one of us ever hated you to begin with. Like I said, everything's changed, and we're working really hard to make it up to you."

He dropped his hand to my books.

"Let him talk to you, Anna," he suggested. "If you still feel the same way after that, then he'll back off. But let him get it out there so that you *know*, all right?"

"Why is he so concerned with making it right?"

"I'm . . . not at liberty to discuss that with you." I tilted my head. "Hey, he's one of my best friends. I can't do that to him."

"Okay, fine."

"The game's Friday night. Why don't you come?"

"I'm still grounded."

"It would mean a lot if you were there."

"It's not like he'll even know . . ." I felt a sense of defeat.

"Oh, he'll know."

"How are you so sure?"

"He's developed this *Anna Radar* in the past few days."

"What?"

He snorted. "He's aware of you, Anna."

"It's not like he can ignore me, Kyle. According to Adam, I take up the full width of the hallway, you know."

"That's not true, and that's definitely not what I meant."

"Then what are you talking about?"

"It's like how I am with Ashley. I'm tuned into her. I know when she's in a room without seeing her enter, I can hear her voice over a group of other people, and whenever I'm next to her, my body is like a live wire."

"That's . . . that's how he is with me?"

"Yeah."

"All right," I relented, holding up my hands. "I'll ask my dad about it tonight."

"That's all I ask of you."

"Liar."

"Yeah, well, that's *my* personal request. If he knew that I asked you, he'd probably kill me."

"How come?"

"He said that you wanted time, and he's trying to give that to you. He told me not to push."

"And that's exactly what you're doing."

"Got me what I wanted though, didn't it?"

"Mm."

"You feel anything for him, Anna?" he asked, his voice low as our other classmates started piling into the room.

I clenched my jaw, nodding stiffly.

He grinned at me. "Then I don't feel bad about it."

"Ass."

"Who means well," he quipped, pointing at me before he turned around to face the front. "And is trying to help out his *friends*."

"I'm a friend now, huh?"

"You always have been." He tilted his head back, looking at me upside down. "I was a sheep, Anna."

"A sheep?"

"You know . . . follow the leader?" I snorted and he grinned again. "Now I want to *be* the leader."

"Oh, Lord help us all."

"You're not very funny."

"I think I'm a riot."

"You would."

I rolled my eyes and gently smacked his forehead. He scowled at me and then winked before sitting up straight. "Friend," he said over his shoulder.

I laughed and looked down at my books again.

"Say it back," he demanded, turning around to face me again.

"What are you, five?"

"Say it!"

"Friend."

He turned back to the front, seemingly satisfied. I snorted and rolled my eyes, grabbing my pen and tapping it against my books.

"That's all I wanted."

"Shut up, Kyle."

I started doodling on the cover of my textbook as Mrs. Leslie called us to attention and took attendance.

He was giving me time. He'd demonstrated that this morning, and he'd told Kyle about it. In fact, it seemed that Kyle knew about it all, and as much as it went against everything I'd ever taught myself, I found myself trusting what he said.

Another thing to add to my list of crazy stuff for the day. Maybe the entire week. Or my entire life.

~*~

On Friday night, I pulled into the parking lot of the school twenty minutes after the game had already started. With my heart in my throat and my hands shaking, I turned off the ignition and looked at the brightly lit baseball field.

My dad, still completely on Evan's side, hadn't hesitated to unground me a day early when I told him what I wanted to do. He'd practically pushed me out the door as soon as dinner was finished and had even threatened to go with me when I told him that I wasn't sure if I should.

Kyle had invited me; Evan hadn't. Maybe he didn't want me there after all. Maybe they were all planning some elaborate hoax on me that would be revealed during halftime. Then all this time I'd spent protecting myself would have been for nothing, and Evan would win.

Throwing caution to the wind, I pushed open the car door and slowly stepped out. I walked out to the field, my heart hammering in my chest when I heard the team shouts from the sidelines. I kept my eyes on the field, walking behind the line of people sitting in canvas camping chairs as I made my way to the side of the bleachers. I stood on my toes to look out onto the field over the fence, trying to see if I could find Evan.

Sighing, I crossed my arms over my chest and leaned against the side of the bleachers. Maybe I'd be able to blend in with the rest of the crowd.

I didn't even know what I came here for. Just because Evan had supposedly developed some kind of radar for me didn't really mean that he wanted me here. Even if he did see me or came over to me, I had no idea what I'd say to him. There really was no reason for me to be here.

I knew what my heart wanted, and I knew what my head was telling me, and neither of them ever agreed with each other. After so long of being the butt of every joke, it was so hard to believe that anyone meant what they said.

Christina and Vince had been the only ones that I could trust and talk to for so long and now that Evan, Kyle and Ashley had been added into the mix, it was as if my entire world was spinning in a different direction. Yesterday at lunch, Christina had told me to give him a chance to explain, and Vince agreed with her. They had both noticed the changes in Evan, and

Vince said Evan had been entirely focused on practice, no longer hanging out with his friends and joking with them.

"Whoever he was on that video, he's not that person anymore," he'd said. "I don't know what you did to him, Anna, but he's done a complete one-eighty."

Vince wouldn't lie to me. I knew that.

So why was I so scared?

"Anna?"

I looked over my shoulder to see Ashley—her camera swinging at her wrist—and Sherri, Evan's sister, walking up with big cups of soda.

"Hey," I said, forcing a smile.

"Come sit with us," Sherri said, grabbing my hand. "Your butt will be numb in five seconds, but you'll be able to see the game."

As Sherri dragged me through the screaming crowd, I tripped over people's feet and just tried to smile and apologize.

"Anna!"

I looked up when I heard Evan's mother, and my breath caught in my throat as Sherri sat down next to her, pulling on my hand and demanding that I sit between them.

"Hi," I managed, smiling awkwardly and sitting down. "It's nice to see you again."

"Hello, Anna." His father peeked around and smiled at me. "How are you?"

I'd only met the man once—when I'd gone to his house after the fight with my father—and he intimidated the hell out of me then. This situation wasn't any better. Who really wants their son's ex-girlfriend sitting with them during a stupid baseball game? This didn't make any sense to me whatsoever.

"Oh, I'm fine," I said. "You?"

"I'd be a lot better if Kyle would hit the . . . Yes!" he yelled, standing up and pumping his fist in the air. "Go, go, go!"

I looked over at Sherri and found that she was on her feet, screaming too. Ashley was cheering as well, her voice rising high above the rest even as she brought the camera up and snapped a few pictures.

"You'll get used to this," Evan's mom said in my ear, her hand on my arm.

"I don't know anything about baseball," I admitted sheepishly.

"That's Kyle, number thirty-four, running toward second base, and that's Evan, number eight, jumping around by the dugout. Those are really the only two you need to focus on."

"How come?"

"Because we're biased." She laughed. "And those are the only two we're really here for anyway."

I looked out to the field.

"He's missed you."

My breath caught in my throat, and I just sat there, not knowing what to say and thinking that coming here was a very bad idea. She patted my arm and leaned away from me, as I numbly watched Evan smack a bat against the sides of his foot.

I sat with his family, watching and trying to join in whenever they screamed and jumped around. We were still winning when our school got its third out, and all the players ran together to change positions.

"We're gonna go and get something to drink," Evan's mom said, stretching. "Do any of you want anything?"

"No, thanks," we all said in unison.

She laughed, grabbing her husband's hand and leading him down the bleachers.

"So, Anna." Ashley leaned back against the abandoned bench behind her and set her empty cup down, "I hear Kyle kind of browbeat you into coming."

I shrugged and laughed nervously, playing with the hem of my shirt.

"He's been pretty miserable," Sherri said, propping her feet up.

"I'm going to talk to him," I said.

"When?"

"I don't know."

"Tonight would be good."

"He's kind of busy."

"The game doesn't last all night, you know."

"I'm just trying to process everything."

"You know the truth, don't you?" Ashley asked. "I gave him those pictures . . ."

"Yes, I know. I just . . . I don't know," I said, leaning forward to twist a strand of my hair around my finger.

"We all make mistakes," Sherri said.

"I *know*."

"All right, enough," Ashley admonished. "Sherri, come with me. I want nachos."

"You want to come, Anna?" she asked as they stood.

"No," I said, sitting up straight. "Thanks."

"Do you want anything?"

"I'm fine, thanks."

"All right. We'll be back."

I wished high school and crushes and feelings weren't always so damn confusing all the time.

~*~

Someone had informed Evan that I was there because as soon as the teams were situated and back in the dugout, Evan popped back out and looked directly at me. I'd wiped my palms on my jeans and tried my best to ignore the fact that his family and Ashley were staring hard at me. We ended up winning the game and everyone rushed the field, hugging, screaming, and laughing as Kyle pranced around in circles. I stayed up in the bleachers, just watching everyone.

I stood and spotted Evan in the crowd, laughing and slapping Vince a high-five; Kyle tackled the both of them and a random baseball went flying in the other direction. I started down the bleachers and stopped at the bottom, not sure whether or not I should go over to them. He seemed like he was in a good mood, and I didn't want to be the one to ruin that. He was with his friends and family, and he was celebrating—I truly had no place there.

Deciding I'd talk to him tomorrow, I turned on my heel, starting in the direction of the parking lot. I dug my keys out of my pocket and played with the key ring as I walked to my car.

I *would* talk to him tomorrow. We'd get through the science fair, and then we'd hash everything out. I wanted to get it all sorted out with him, and if that meant staying up half the night—*oh, Dad will* love *that*—then I'd do it. He'd wormed his way into my heart at some point, and dammit if I didn't want him back there.

"Anna!"

I turned to see Evan running toward me, the sound of his cleats obnoxiously hitting the pavement. I stopped and fidgeted with my key ring again as he stopped in front of me.

"Hey," he said, breathless.

Fourteen

"Hi. Uh, congrats on the win," I said, nervously biting the inside of my cheek. "You did really well."

"Thanks. Are you leaving?"

"Yeah."

"Oh. I, uh . . . I'm sorry that Kyle asked you to come . . ."

"Please don't be."

"I told him to leave you alone until . . . but he's just . . ."

"It's okay."

He looked down at the ground, shifting from foot to foot as he rubbed the back of his neck.

"You were . . . your family is inside, Evan, what are you doing out here with me?" I jingled my keys in my hand.

"I see them all the time." He reached out his hand and then dropped it again, shifting uncomfortably. "I don't see you enough."

"You see me plenty in school."

He just tilted his head and looked down at his feet.

"Is this . . . are you really done with me?"

"No," I said, looking down at my feet. "We just need to talk."

"What about tonight?"

"You just had a game, Evan. You've got to be exhausted."

He shrugged. "I'm still pumped, actually. Adrenaline high. If you don't want to, that's fine. I just thought that maybe since you were already here, and we're kind of already talking that we could . . . not stop?"

"You really want to do this tonight?"

"Tonight. Yesterday. Last Saturday morning." I tilted my head, and he shrugged, laughing nervously. "It's true."

"Okay, fine."

"Seriously?"

"*Grey's*?"

"*Grey's*," he confirmed.

"And yes, seriously," I added.

"Did you want to wait or did you want to meet somewhere else?"

"Come to the playground," I suggested. "It's on Hunter Street."

"No crawling through the woods this time, huh?"

"I figured that you've had your fill of seeing imaginary snakes and feeling imaginary furry things, so . . ."

"I appreciate that."

"You're welcome," I said with a small smile.

"I'll uh . . . I'll meet you there, then?" he asked, rocking back and forth on his heels.

"Yeah."

"I won't be long. Was there a certain time that you needed to be home?"

"I'll stop by my house and tell my dad. See what time he wants me back."

"I'll hurry."

I looked down at my feet. "All right."

"I'll see you soon."

I was just about to walk away when he took my arm, turned me around, and brushed his lips across my cheek.

"Thank you, Anna," he whispered.

"Yeah," I said. My voice broke as I took a step back from him. "Hunter Street."

"Got it."

He turned and ran toward the school, and I breathed a heavy sigh before going to my car. I climbed in, drove back to my house, and left the car running as I went inside. My dad was sitting on the couch, the coffee table covered with papers with a pen tucked behind his ear. He looked over at me once before patting the papers in front of him, looking for the pen.

"How was the game?"

I walked over to him, took the pen from his ear, and handed it to him. He chuckled and dropped it on the table.

"We won. Uh, I'm gonna meet Evan out at the playground," I said, clearing my throat.

He stared at me.

"Midnight," he said as he picked up the pen.

"Thanks."

"Yep."

Well, at least we were making a little bit of progress. It was taking time, and it wasn't a complete one hundred percent father-daughter relationship, but it was a tiny bit better than it had been. I got to the empty playground and walked over to the merry-go-round to sit between the bars; it creaked as I pushed myself.

This was my chance to ask him *everything* I didn't understand, and all I felt was an all-encompassing fear. I wanted to know the answers to everything I'd been wondering about, but I was afraid all my fears would be realized. That this was just a joke, he had only been kidding, and I meant less to him than I did before. Though he'd consistently tried to make contact with me since the party, it was still so hard to comprehend that he'd changed *this much* over three weeks' time. It was so hard to comprehend that he'd changed this much because of *me*.

Headlights suddenly appeared, and I watched Evan park his car behind mine. The headlights died out, and the sound of his car door slamming echoed in the quiet neighborhood. I took yet another deep breath and set my feet firmly on the ground, stopping the motion of the merry-go-round and waiting for him to appear.

He approached, keys jingling as they hung from his hand. "Hey," he said, stopping in front of me.

"Hi." I indicated the empty space next to me. "Care to join me?"

He sat down, dropping his keys on the space next to him.

"Can I explain it all to you now?" he asked, folding his hands in his lap.

I closed my eyes and, laid down on the hard surface, my legs still dangling off the side. Then I raised my legs and placed my feet flat on the edge.

"Yeah."

"You know that Steve throws these parties whenever his parents are out of town, and I always used to go to them. It was just common knowledge that I'd attend, and I never disappointed. Grace took the video; I thought she was only taking a picture. I was drunk, and I was on my way to being pretty damn high, and I didn't . . . I didn't *know you*."

"Do you think—?"

"Please just let me finish?" he pled.

"Fine." I kept my eyes closed. "We were being assholes, and Steve asked me that just because it was when we were first paired up for the project, and it was a fun topic for us."

I flinched, crossing my arms over my stomach.

"His parents bought him his BMW a few days after the party, and he hasn't driven the Buick since. I had to throw out those boots from the video because I'd worn the soles off them. That's what I was trying to tell you in class the other day."

"I know that now," I said. "It doesn't change the fact that you still said those things."

"I know that. I wasn't . . . Anna, I'm not the same person now."

"What changed?"

"When I grabbed you that day, and I put marks on you . . . Jesus Christ, Anna, that was like my fucking wake-up call or something. I was raised to respect women and treat them as queens and to *never* put my hands on them that way."

He stayed quiet, and I finally opened my eyes, staring up at the star-specked sky as I thought of what to say.

"My dad, Zack, isn't my biological father."

Through the dim beam of the streetlights, I could see the muscles in his back tense as he pushed us.

"What?"

"My real father abused my mother." He looked over his shoulder at me, and the pain on his face nearly took my breath away. "He hit me once when I was three, and that was what it took for Mom to call the police on him. I'd always said I'd never be that way to anyone, no matter what. And I . . ." He looked away from me. "My first memory is of him coming at me and hitting me as I sat on the living room floor with a coloring book while my mom screamed at him, and I just . . . I *hurt* you. I put *marks* on you like he did to me and my mother and . . ."

I felt him stiffen as I got up and sat down behind him, pressed myself against his back, and wrapped my arms around his waist, while I rested my cheek on his back.

It didn't make the things he'd said about me right, and it didn't get him off the hook completely, but it sure as hell helped me understand a lot more about him. Not everything was as perfect and as peachy in his life as he'd made it seem, either.

"Anna, it's not an excuse to get you to believe me."

"I know," I whispered, tilting my head up and resting my chin on his back. "I know."

"I'm so sorry."

"Evan, please, you were already forgiven for that."

"When I said those things, . . . I . . . I had no right to say them. No one has any right to say anything about you, and it took me hurting you to realize that. I don't deserve your forgiveness, and I don't deserve your company. What I deserve is for you to kick me to the curb and make me suffer for everything I've ever done to you."

"I would never do that."

"But you should!" he exclaimed, pulling my arms from his waist and jumping up to pace in front of me. "God, you *should*."

"But I won't."

"Why?"

"Everyone deserves a second chance."

"I've already had my second chance with you, remember?"

"*This you* hasn't had a second chance with me. *This you* is different than the guy I talked to three weeks ago."

He stared at me, and I stared back, doing my best to think of anything else to say to him. I'd never expected to hear something like this from him and wondered why we had never talked about his past before. It was a small town and people couldn't keep their mouths shut about crap like this.

"Why didn't I know about your dad before?"

"Your father actually made sure to keep it quiet for us. The only people that knew were the neighbors who saw the cops show up, and the cops themselves."

"How did my dad—"

"My mom needed a lawyer, and since this is such a 'big town' and all, it didn't take much convincing on your dad's part to ask the police to keep it quiet." He shrugged and smiled sadly at me, shoving his hands in his pockets.

"The neighbors didn't say anything?"

"The neighbors were Kyle's family and Zack."

Well, that explained everything. "Oh."

"Yeah."

"You always refer to Zack as your father . . ."

"He may not be my biological father, but he's always been there when I needed him. He's more of a father to me than Greg was, and that's all that matters to me."

I curled my legs underneath me and stared down at my lap as I fidgeted.

"When did your feelings for me change?" I asked. "When did you want to be with me?"

"When I came to see you after Brittany and Grace wrote those things on your locker. When you let me get you out of the house and trusted me when I asked you to."

"Why?"

"You are such a good person, Anna," he said. "When I saw what had happened to your locker, I just . . . I saw red." He chuckled darkly. "You're funny and sweet, and you've got more personality than anyone I used to call friend. You've never tried to fit in, you've never asked for anything from anyone, you've never *bothered* anyone, and all we did was torture you. It took that incident for me to really get it."

"I'm not thin, Evan. I probably never will be."

"I don't fucking care about that."

"You used to."

"I used to care about a lot of shit that I don't anymore. Anna," he said, taking a step forward and crouching down in front of me, "You're beautiful. I meant it when I said it before, and I mean it just as much now. Everything about you is beautiful, and I'm sorry for everything."

"If I say that you're forgiven, will you stop apologizing?" I asked.

"Yes."

"You're forgiven."

"You're not just saying that out of pity?"

"Evan . . ."

"I'm serious."

"So am I."

"Do you believe me about the pictures and the party?"

"Yes."

"Do you hate me?"

"What? No!"

"You should."

"Evan."

"I mean it!"

"I thought you were trying to get me back?"

"I'm just trying to make things right."

"What do you think you just did?"

"I don't know."

I snorted.

"There aren't any more videos, are there?"

"I'm honestly not sure. And if there are, they are not recent."

"I'm sorry for not trusting you and not listening to you."

"I wouldn't have trusted me, either. You're not at fault here, Anna."

"We'll get through it." I leaned over and grabbed his hand, holding it tightly. "High school doesn't last forever."

"Thank fucking God for that."

"Amen."

He laughed weakly, and I tugged on his hand. He stood, and I pulled him back down to sit in front of me. He slid his knees onto the platform, and he grabbed onto one of the bars.

"I want to try again with you," he whispered, resting his head against the bar behind him. "If you'll let me, I want to try again."

"What do you think we're doing right now?"

"Sitting here while I pour my pathetic heart out to you and beg you to take me back?"

I laughed and twisted our fingers together, bringing the back of his hand to my cheek. He trailed his knuckles down my cheek, and then dropped our hands to my lap.

"I'm going to make mistakes," he said.

"So am I. And we'll figure them out together, Evan. This isn't something we have to be perfect at."

"You're so much smarter than I am," he whispered, chuckling.

"Yeah, well . . ."

His mouth dropped open, and I laughed, throwing my head back and then shrieking when he tackled me. He hovered over me, a crooked smile on his face as he anchored his elbows on either side of my head.

"You said it!" I exclaimed.

"You weren't supposed to *agree* to it."

"I cannot tell a lie."

"All right, George."

I laughed and placed my hands on his chest, feeling his erratic heartbeat underneath my palm.

"You make that happen," he whispered.

I met his eyes.

"What?"

"You're the only one who could make my heart beat that fast." He chuckled, looking away. "Whenever you're around me . . ."

"Anna Radar?"

"Kyle," he said, dropping his forehead to my shoulder.

I wrapped my hands around his shoulders and closed my eyes when he buried his nose in my neck.

"Can I ask you something?" I said cautiously.

"Anything."

"Were you ever embarrassed to have me meet your family?" I waited anxiously, dreading his answer.

"When we first had to do this project, yes," he said. "But the more we talked, and the more I got to know you . . . it just didn't matter anymore."

"And then I showed up on your driveway."

"Something like that."

"Was it Brittany and Grace that put the DVD on my doorstep?"

"Yes."

I grunted, and he lifted his head.

"They've been taken care of."

"You didn't fracture their jaws too, did you?"

"No!" He laughed. "Ashley took care of it."

"How?"

"Aside from Mrs. Gold, she's yearbook advisor. She's also very crafty when it comes to using Photoshop."

"What would she—"

"You don't want to know."

"Alright."

"What do you say, Anna?" he asked, gently nudging his nose against mine. "You want to be my girlfriend again?"

"I *suppose* so." I sighed dramatically. He looked like I'd just kicked his puppy. "Joke, joking. Too soon? Crap. Sorry."

I placed my hands on his cheeks, rubbing my thumbs underneath his eyes. "*Really* sorry." He turned his head into my palm, pressing his lips to the center and raising his hand to cover mine.

I buried my other hand in his hair, silently counting the times he kissed my palm.

"Yes, by the way."

He laughed, kissing my palm for like the eighteenth time before wrapping his fingers around my hand and looking back down at me.

"I'm different," he said.

"I know."

"So . . . can I kiss you whenever I want?"

"If you really want to."

"I really want to."

"Then what are you waiting for?"

He smiled gently. "You."

"I'm trapped underneath you. I'm clearly not going anywhere."

"Do you want me to move?"

"No, I'm fine."

"Then stop complaining."

"Are you going to get to the kissing sometime tonight, or do I need to go home?"

"I'm not sure I'd like that."

"Well then get to it!"

He leaned down, kissing me at last.

"I've missed you," he whispered, pulling back from me slightly.

"I've heard."

"Fucking Kyle."

"Your mother."

"*What?*"

"She said it at the game. You know, you talk a lot for someone who supposedly wanted to kiss me."

"My *mother* told you that I missed you?"

"Yes."

"Well hell."

"Sherri said you were miserable."

He groaned and buried his face back in my neck. I laughed and wrapped my arms tightly around his neck, closing my eyes and turning my head to brush my nose against his cheek.

"Traitors."

"Were they right?"

"Doesn't matter."

"If it makes you feel any better, I wasn't so great without you, either."

He grinned. "That makes it a little better."

"That's what I thought."

"Think you're a know-it-all."

"Are you disagreeing?"

He pouted. "No."

"All right then."

"What time do you need to be home?"

"Midnight."

He raised his arm, presumably looking at the watch I never realized he wore.

"Good," he said brightly. "I've got half an hour to make out with you."

I rolled with laughter until he silenced me with a kiss. So we spent the next half-hour making out on a merry-go-round at a children's playground. Afterward, we walked to my car, holding hands as we talked about the science fair and what time we needed to be there to set up. Not that we had all that much to set up to begin with, but it would give us plenty of time to get the last minute details into place.

"Do you want me to pick you up?" he asked, opening my door for me.

"If you want to."

"I do."

"Then I guess, yes."

"You're going to make things difficult, huh?"

"I never said I was easy."

He laughed and I groaned, pushing on his shoulder and climbed into my car. He yanked me back, wrapping his arms around my shoulders when I fell into him.

"I wouldn't have you any other way."

I smiled and leaned back into him.

Size fourteen be damned; I'd never felt more accepted and more hopeful than I was right now. And I wasn't even scared. For once in my entire life, I felt content with myself, and there was nothing more that I needed.

Epilogue

"**Tell me again why we're here,**" I said, staring at the front of Collins Point High School from the car.

"So that we can see how horrible everyone else looks."

I looked over at him, raising my eyebrow as he grinned at me.

"This place is like hell. No, it's worse than that. It's the seventh circle of hell."

"You're quite the drama queen tonight."

"I hate everyone in there."

"You hate Kyle and Ashley? Christina and Vince?"

I glared at him, and he laughed and grabbed my hand. I looked back at the front of the school and scowled.

Nothing had changed. It was just as I remembered it from ten years ago. As if time had just stopped in this part of the world, and I wasn't sure whether I wanted to be sick or enjoy the memories of my senior year that rushed back to me.

"This is going to be fine."

"I feel like I'm seventeen again."

"But you're not."

"Well I feel like it!"

"Anna." He laughed, leaning over to gently kiss my cheek. "You are a beautiful, successful, smart wife and mother. You're still that strong, independent woman who graduated with me ten years ago. There is absolutely no reason for you to be worried."

"These people—"

"Won't even recognize you." He grabbed my chin and turned my head, gently kissing me. "Relax, sweetheart."

I placed my hand against his heart. That had continued to be our thing through our entire relationship. When either of us needed reassurance, feeling the other's heartbeat always made everything make sense again.

I'd been dreading our high school reunion ever since we'd received the invitations in the mail. I'd even gone so far as to beg Evan to rip it up and forget about the whole thing. But he had to be a sadistic bastard and insist that we go no matter what I said to him.

His acceptance letter arrived a few days after the science fair—it had apparently made a detour and was delivered to a Mr. Ericsson at the retirement community across town— and we spent the rest of the night celebrating with our friends. It was hard to believe that it had already been ten years since then.

We stayed in New York after we graduated, both of us having fallen in love with all the ways that it was different from Collins Point. It had the added advantage of not having a single person from our graduating class follow us there.

We'd worked through most of our schooling and ended up with two jobs a piece after we'd graduated, neither of us using our degrees at the time. It had seemed nearly impossible to find a job in either of our fields, no matter how many places we'd sent our resumes to—or, in Evan's case, samples. Then Evan had received a call from the New York Times at the end of March, and I'd finally found a practice willing to take me under their wing. As soon as we'd had enough money, the first thing we did was get married.

Our relationship had had its ups and downs—boys at college weren't as narrow-minded as the ones back in Collins Point, and I'd found that having a jealous boyfriend was equally flattering and annoying as hell.

Not to say that Mr. Gorgeous didn't have his own fair share of obsessed stalkers following his fine ass around campus, but I'd expected that. He still spent most nights sneaking into my dorm, after all, so there really was no reason to worry—he'd spent an entire day asking me why it didn't bother me. I said I trusted him; he took it the wrong way and thought I meant that he didn't trust me. That was our first big fight; we spent a week without seeing or speaking to each other before I found him camped outside my dorm room one night after class with his head in his hands and about ten dozen roses at his feet.

Now, even when we were angry at each other, we at least still slept in the same bed. Makeup sex was a really wonderful thing, too. It also resulted in our first child.

Evan and I had talked about having kids and had decided that when it happened, it happened. I'd stopped taking my birth control pills, and we both did our best not to rush to the drugstore and buy a test every time we made love.

We'd been married for almost two years, living in a beautiful brownstone in the better part of the city, when I finally realized that I didn't have the flu. The first thing I did was call Evan, and he'd rushed home from work, three different pregnancy tests in his hand. They had all been positive, but we'd made an appointment with the doctor just to be sure.

Macie Corrine Drake was the spitting image of her father, and she had the smart-ass attitude to go with it. Her eyes were green like mine, her hair was brown like her father's, and we absolutely adored her.

Now we had a beautiful four-year-old baby girl visiting with her Grandpa Bruce while we sat in front of the one place in the world I despised the most.

"I'm not in a position to relax," I said, gritting my teeth.

"You're not doing anything good for my son in this condition, you know."

His hand trailed from my chin and rested on my swollen stomach, as he rubbed it. I sighed and placed my hand over his, linking our fingers and closing my eyes as I concentrated on breathing evenly.

"We don't have to stay long," he whispered, resting his chin on my shoulder and kissing my neck. "Go in, see how horrible the rest of our class looks, and then we can be off."

"We promised everyone dinner tonight."

"So we did."

"You're a pain in my ass."

"You love me."

"Your mother paid me to love you."

"Is that any way to speak to the father of your children?"

"Who says the kids are yours? They could be the milkman's."

He laughed and kissed me. "We don't have a milkman."

"That *you* know of."

"Macie looks too much like me." He grinned. "Maybe this baby will look just like you."

"God help him."

"Going back to that place again, are we?"

My self-esteem had been low for eighteen years of my life, and Evan had made it his mission in life to raise it. It had been working well until we pulled into the parking lot of this place. I felt like that same girl I'd been while I was there. Pregnancy hormones didn't help this situation, either.

I'd gotten down to a size eight after Macie was born, thrilled that I hadn't kept the weight from my pregnancy and had somehow managed to lose a little more. Evan hadn't been so thrilled about it, pouting when I modeled a new pair of jeans for him. I squealed that I'd never been this small in my life.

He'd told me that I was perfect no matter what size I was—as he often had in the past—and had confessed that he even liked it more when I was heavier. I'd loved him for it but had done my best to keep off the weight. It had worked for a while, until he started bringing home chocolate donuts and cheesecake from my favorite diner in the heart of Manhattan and had never been able to resist.

A month later, I was buying size twelve jeans, which still made me happy—kind of—because again, the smallest size I'd ever been before Macie showed up was a fourteen. I'd made him promise to stop bringing home that crap if I stopped trying to be thinner, and he'd agreed. Now, four years later and pregnant, I felt like a whale. Granted, it was for a good reason, but showing up to my ten-year high school reunion bigger than ever made me want to hide in the car for the rest of the night.

"I can't help it," I whined, burying my head in his chest.

"Okay, listen," he said, wrapping his arms around my shoulders, "this is gonna be a piece of cake, babycakes."

"Babycakes?" I asked.

"Don't question it."

"Can I call you cupcake?"

"You can call me anything you want if it gets you out of this car."

"In public?"

"Will you get out of the car?"

"Possibly."

"You do know that Kyle will probably tear off the car door in an attempt to get you out of it, don't you?"

"He doesn't know what car we drive."

"No, but I'm pretty sure it's safe to say that we're the only two still sitting in ours."

"There's a lot of people here. It'll take him a while."

"No, it won't."

"Why did we need to come here again?"

"I already told you." He laughed, threading his hand through my hair. "We're going to see all of our old classmates at their worst."

"Or their best."

"You're way too negative for your own good."

"You knew this when you married me."

"What do I have to do to make you see that none of it matters?" he whispered, trailing his hand down to my stomach. "The only things that matter are you, me, Macie, this little guy, our families, and our friends. These other people haven't mattered to us in over ten years, Anna. Don't give them the satisfaction of thinking that they do."

I sat back and placed both of my hands over his on my stomach.

"You're right."

"I know it."

I rolled my eyes and he laughed, leaning over to kiss me again.

"Stay here."

"It's not like I'm going to go very far."

He narrowed one eye at me, and I grinned, leaning back in my seat as he climbed out of the car. I tapped my fingers against my stomach, looking down and rubbing it.

"I hope you're like your father, little guy," I whispered, smiling when I felt him kick. "He needs some support keeping your momma sane."

I looked up when my door opened and smiled at Evan, placing my hand in his. He helped me out of the car, closed it, and wrapped an arm around my waist, placing the other on my stomach again.

"Your momma keeps your papa sane, too," he murmured, leaning down and pressing a kiss on my abdomen.

My eyes watered, and I looked up at him as he stood up straight. Flinging my arms around his neck, I kissed his jaw reverently.

"I love you so much." I sniffled, burying my face into his shirt.

He chuckled and wrapped his arms around me, hugging me and kissing my temple.

"I love you too, babycakes."

I snorted and wiped my eyes on my shirtsleeve. I wound my fingers through his when he grabbed my hand.

"Cupcake," I retorted, sniffling.

"Yours."

I blew out a deep breath, squeezed his hand, and looked up at the school again.

"Okay," I said. "Let's get this over with."

"It won't be that bad, I promise."

He winked before leading me to the front doors, each footstep echoing in my head as we stepped closer to the entrance.

"And if it is?" I asked as I pulled him to a stop in front of the doors.

"I give you full permission to name our son Jameson."

About a month after Macie was born, Evan had gone out with some friends as a celebration of becoming a father and had gotten completely hammered. He'd been drinking Jameson whiskey and upon his return home, he kept telling me that he loved the name *Jameson* and wanted to name our future son after the whiskey; that night, he was determined that we were going to have a son. When I reminded him of that the next morning while his head was in the toilet, he'd told me if I did that, he'd divorce me.

"Done."

He kissed my cheek as he pushed open the door for me.

"You're going to lose," he whispered, placing his hand on the small of my back.

"I hope I do."

We walked into the lobby of the gymnasium, and I wasn't sure whether to laugh or turn around and run back to the car when I realized that time really *had* stood still. A part from a few additions—a snack machine in the corner and a display case at end of the room—everything was the same. It even smelled the same.

"Relax, babycakes."

I grunted and he laughed, leading me up to the table near the gym doors. I sighed as I spotted my nametag, *Weller* typed in bold letters after *Arianna*. I tilted my head, vaguely aware of Evan grabbing his own nametag and saying something to me.

That wasn't right. I wasn't a Weller anymore, and I definitely wasn't Arianna.

"Give me your pen," I said, holding out one hand as I grabbed the nametag with the other.

"Why?"

"Please?"

He grabbed a pen from his jacket pocket. Ever since he'd gotten his own column a few years ago, he'd taken to carrying one around with him almost religiously. When I suggested buying some kind of electronic device that would make things a little easier for him, he'd immediately shot my idea down by saying that he didn't trust his brilliant ideas to technology.

I rested my nametag on my stomach—one of the advantages of being seven months pregnant—and scribbled out *Arianna Weller*, writing *Anna Drake* underneath it. I smiled down at it before handing Evan his pen back and pinning the tag to my shirt. I looked at him and grinned.

"Want to explain that?" he asked, sticking the pen back in his pocket.

"I'm not that girl anymore."

"You're still you, Anna."

"I'm your wife; I've been that way for six years, and I'm going to be that way for the rest of our lives." I linked my fingers with his again. "I'm someone different and better thanks to you."

He stared at me before leaning down and kissing me forcefully. He cupped the back of my head until I stepped into him and placed our hands on my stomach.

"Fuck, I love you," he said as he pulled away from me.

I smiled, keeping my eyes closed as he rested his forehead against mine.

"I love you too." I squared my shoulders as I opened my eyes. I looked over at the gym doors and squeezed his hand. "Let's go in there."

"There she is," he whispered into my ear, placing a quick kiss on my cheek before he stepped ahead of me and opened the door.

I took a deep breath and followed him inside, finding that the gym was only half-full of classmates I barely recognized who stood around, talking and comparing life stories with drinks in their hands and dressed to the nines.

I know for a fact that the majority of them still lived in the same town, so the odds that most of the people here didn't still know each other's business was very slim. If they wanted to pretend that they hadn't seen each other in the past twenty-four hours, hey, who was I to call them out on it?

"Oh Jesus Christ, it's about time." Ashley popped up at my side and placed her hand on my shoulder. "Kyle was about to go and find you."

"Told you," Evan whispered into my ear.

"Shut up."

"Come on!" she exclaimed, grabbing my arm and leading us to their table.

"Anna!" Christina squealed, jumping up and wrapping her arms around my neck.

I laughed and hugged her back as much as possible. We hadn't been able to see everyone when we got in yesterday afternoon, having been whisked away by Evan's parents for some family bonding and sleep to recover from the three-hour drive with a four-year old. Ashley and Kyle had shown up sometime around eight and demanded that we go out to a late dinner with them, declaring that they had first dibs with us for some unknown reason.

Ashley and Kyle had stayed close to home, relocating to Schenectady and starting a joint remodeling business that had taken off very well. Vince and Christina had moved out to California, where Vince was a successful agent and Christina was a publicist for a few relatively unknown celebrities. Our friends had flourished, and I'd missed them horribly.

"Hi!" I squealed back, squeezing her tightly.

"How's the little peanut?" she immediately asked, bending down to rest her hands on my stomach and place her ear over my bellybutton. "Everything all right in there?"

Evan laughed and kissed my cheek before going over to slap Vince on the shoulder and Kyle on the back of the head.

"Everything is fine in there," I assured her, plopping down into one of the uncomfortable plastic chairs as she stood.

"How's the little princess?" Ashley asked, already sitting down and leaning her elbow on the table next to me.

We'd split up the Godparent thing between our friends—Vince and Christina were Macie's godparents, and Ashley and Kyle were our as-yet-unnamed baby boy's. All of them spoiled the hell out of Macie as it was, and I was sure nothing would change when our little boy showed up in two months.

"She's good. Visiting with my dad tonight."

The relationship between my father and I had improved over the years. I found that we really could get along, and had actually found myself missing his company while I was in college. Evan, Macie, and I talked to him on the phone every Friday night at seven—Thursday nights were *Hell's Hospital* nights and as much as Evan complained about it, he still sat and watched it with me—and my father and I had gotten along better than we ever had.

Apparently, distance had been the thing we'd needed the most.

"I'd better see that beautiful girl before you guys leave," Christina said, pointing at me.

"Promise. How's Calvin?"

"Growing up so fast." She grinned, her eyes sparking at the mention of her and Vince's only son.

He was six and an absolute gentleman. Between Christina and her manners, and Vince and his need to teach his son everything there was to know about sports, he was well versed in all things that mattered. Then, of course, there were the superheroes, comic books, and Disney-Pixar movies that every kid loved. When we visited, Macie and he had spent at least half of that time watching movies and then imitating everything they'd seen when it was over.

"I know what you mean." Ashley laughed. "The twins are almost four and it seems like just yesterday, I was in labor."

I remembered hearing about all of it. Macie had only been a few months old when Ashley announced that she was pregnant, and it had only taken a few months after that to find out that she was pregnant with twins. Darla and Christine Mahon were the most energetic kids I'd ever known. They'd definitely gotten their personalities and energy from their father, while their looks were all from Ashley. The two of them were going to have their hands full when they got older and started dating, though Kyle had already declared they'd never date, much less get older.

Evan and I were Calvin's godparents, and Darla and Christine's godparents were Kyle's brother and sister-in-law.

"Are we not good enough for you, Anna?"

I looked across the table to see Vince pouting, his bottom lip shoved out so far he could probably wrap it up around his head if he so desired. I laughed and waved him over to me, holding out my arms as he bent down and hugged me.

"You feeling okay?" he asked as he pulled back and bent down in between Christina and me.

"Totally stressed out."

He laughed and patted my knee.

"That's not good for the little man in there."

"So I've heard."

"Fuck 'em all," he grinned, standing up again and kissing my cheek.

"You're gorgeous."

"I tell her that, and she refuses to believe me tonight," Evan said, matter-of-factly.

I scrunched my nose and stuck my tongue out at him. He laughed and grabbed a chair, pulling it up behind me and draping his arm over my shoulders.

We talked without interruption, Ashley pointing out people such as Brittany Feldman, who had been managing the local hardware shop for the past five years, and Grace Alcott, who had moved out to Hollywood and hadn't been able to land more than a few commercials here and there.

Steve Forrester, dragging a stick-thin blonde around the middle of the floor, still looked like he had in high school. He'd taken over his parents' construction business and seemed to think that he owned the world because of it. Adam Laveque hadn't appeared yet, but his alcoholism had been common knowledge around Collins Point for about four years now, or so I'd been told. Other classmates that I barely knew had stopped at our table to say hello, spouting on about their lives and sliding away when someone else called their name.

"Evan!"

We both looked in the direction when we heard a voice that I'd tried to forget, and I cringed, placing my hands protectively over my stomach as Grace walked up to us. She was carting around a guy that looked like he might've just graduated high school, and was doing everything in her power to show off the ring on her left hand.

"Hello, Grace," Evan said coolly. "How've you been?"

"Fabulous!" she said in a sing-song voice, waving her left hand at him.

I looked behind me at Ashley who rolled her eyes. I laughed and looked over at Christina who was mimicking Grace's hand movements.

"This is Antoine," she proudly announced, gripping the guy's hand. "We're engaged."

"Never would've known," I heard Ashley mumble.

I pressed my lips together, clearing my throat and looking down at my stomach in an attempt not to laugh at her.

"Congratulations," Evan said, coughing and grabbing my hand. I looked over at him and smiled, squeezing his hand before I looked up at Grace again. "You remember Anna, don't you Grace?"

Her gaze slowly shifted as she appraised me. "Arianna Weller?"

"Hello, Grace," I said through my teeth in an attempt to be polite.

Fourteen

"You still hang around with her?" she asked, crossing one arm under her breasts and jutting a thumb at me. "I thought you would've grown out of that years ago."

"They're married, half-wit," Ashley snapped, slapping her hand on the table. "Where have you been for six years? Collins Point is not that big of a town, so don't be a dumbass and pretend that you didn't know."

Christina choked on her drink, fanning herself as she gasped for air.

"Nice to see you again, Ashley," Grace said dryly.

"I wish I could say the same to you."

"Well, we have to get going," Grace said, turning on her heel before any of us could say anything more.

"Damn!" Kyle said, his voice booming. "I thought she was a moron back in high school. She hasn't changed much, has she?"

"No." I laughed and saw her smack Antoine's arm as they stormed over to their table.

We continued talking about all the ways our kids annoyed and amused us, briefly mentioning our careers and pretty much ignoring the rest of our classmates.

Brittany had meekly made her way over to us, being as polite and nice as anyone else. She'd gotten divorced from Steve three years ago, she'd said, and he'd given up the rights to their daughter. The blonde he was carting around was their former nanny, and it was hard to hold a grudge against someone who had to watch her ex-husband troll around the room with someone else.

I made her sit with us, and we spent the rest of the evening at our little round table, sharing stories. By the end of the night, I was exhausted and more than ready to go home as opposed to going out to the dinner we'd promised everyone else.

"You okay, babycakes?" Evan whispered into my ear, trailing his hand up and down my arm.

"Are you going to make that nickname permanent?"

"I'm thinking that I kind of like it, so yeah, probably."

I laughed, leaning my head against his and smiling when he pressed a soft kiss against my ear.

"We're here for another couple of days," he whispered, nuzzling his nose into my hair. "We can go out to dinner with them tomorrow night if you want."

"Will they be okay with that?"

"They have to be. Plus," he began, his other hand trailing back to my stomach, "you have a pretty good excuse."

"Our son is not an excuse."

"No, but if you're tired, they'll all understand. You can't overexert yourself, baby."

"I've missed everyone." I pouted, closing my eyes.

He laughed as he kissed my temple. "I know. I have, too. But like I said, we have a few more days. It's not a big deal."

I opened my eyes and blinked a few times to readjust to the harsh lighting of the gym.

"What are you naming him?" Brittany asked from her spot in between Christina and me.

I looked over at her and smiled, placing my hand over Evan's.

He said, "We're not—"

"I was thinking William," I interrupted. "After his amazing, wonderful papa."

He looked down at me, shock clearly written all over his face, and I smiled and placed my hand on his cheek, rubbing my thumb over his chin.

I'd been thinking about it a lot and while he'd already told me that he didn't want any son of ours named after him directly, I had been sitting on his middle name ever since we found out that we were having a boy. He hadn't brought up the name issue until recently, and I had wanted it to be a surprise. Being here tonight, it just seemed like the perfect place to tell him.

"You . . ."

"Is that okay?" I asked when he continued to stare at me.

"You are . . ." He chuckled. "You're perfect for me; you know that, don't you?"

"Is that your middle name, Evan?" Brittany asked, bringing me out of my private moment with Evan.

"Yeah," he said, not breaking his gaze with me. "It was my grandfather's name."

"You're okay with that?"

"I'm more than okay with that, Anna. Fuck," he whispered, standing and pulling me up with him. He wrapped his arms as far around me as he could and buried his face into my hair. "You are . . . I have no words for you."

I smiled and wrapped my arms around his neck, resting my forehead on his shoulder and closing my eyes again.

"Let's leave. Right now," he whispered into my ear, gently kissing my neck. "I need you, Anna."

I tangled my hand in his hair, pressing a kiss against his jaw.

"Yeah."

"We're gonna get going," he said, looking at our table of friends. "Can we postpone dinner until tomorrow night?"

"You all right, Anna?" Kyle asked, tilting his head at me and draping an arm over the back of Ashley's chair.

"Yeah, just kind of tired," I said, picking my head up to look at him. "It's been a long day."

"Tomorrow night for sure," Christina said, pointing at me. "We only have a few days."

"Promise."

"Get some sleep, Anna." Ashley smiled, winking at me.

I laughed, hugging everyone including Brittany. She seemed shocked and hugged me back tightly.

"I'm sorry about what happened when we were in school, Anna," she said.

I grinned and grabbed her hand.

"It's okay. We were all pretty stupid back then."

She smiled and squeezed my hand.

"Did you want to come tomorrow?"

"Oh, Mel doesn't do well in restaurants." She laughed sheepishly and fidgeted in her seat, referencing her daughter. "Thank-you, though."

"If you change your mind, we're staying at Evan's parents' place. You can reach us there."

She smiled at me. "Thank you, Anna."

"You're welcome."

"Early lunch!" Ashley declared, pointing at us as I dropped Brittany's hand. "Well, not really early, but lunch. Twelve o'clock at the diner for old time's sake."

"All right." Evan wrapped his arm around my waist. "We'll see you then."

With another round of good-byes and one more invite extended to Brittany, we were finally walking out of the gymnasium. It was barely nine when we finally made it back to his parents' house, and my heart jumped when the only light on in the entire place was the front porch. Macie was staying with my dad, and Evan's parents had a completely separate floor all to themselves.

Evan led me into the house and locked the doors behind us, leading me to his old bedroom on the first floor. He closed the door and turned to me, pulling me into his arms. He kissed me slowly, twining our fingers together and walking me toward his old double bed. We did everything slowly—undressing each other, kissing, touching, making love to each other, and whispering quiet words of adoration and love. When we were done, he stretched out beside me, tracing invisible patterns on my stomach and pressing soft kisses against my shoulder blades.

"Sometimes this doesn't seem real." I placed one hand on his wrist and folded the other underneath my head.

"What doesn't?"

"You, me . . . Macie and this baby. I never thought I'd ever be lucky enough to have all of this."

"All of what?"

"This life with you."

"If anything, it's the other way around," he whispered, resting his chin on my shoulder. "Coming back here reminds me that I didn't deserve any chances with you, and you gave them to me anyway. I'm a very lucky man."

I turned over, and Evan moved back a little, placing his hand on my stomach again when I'd settled in front of him. "You gave me a chance, too," I said placing a hand on his cheek. "You didn't let me push you away, and you fought for me when it mattered most."

"You were more than worth it."

"So were you. You still are."

He leaned down and gently kissed me. I laughed as the baby kicked right under his hand, and I rubbed my thumb over the bridge of his nose as he pulled away from me.

"Hope you didn't mind all that bouncing your momma just did," Evan teased, scooting down in the bed and placing gentle kisses against my bellybutton.

"Yeah, your papa apparently *needed* me or something," I said dramatically, putting my hand over his.

"Oh, but your momma wasn't complaining now, was she?" he cooed, still pressing small kisses around my stomach.

"Your papa failed to mention that he had his tongue down my throat."

"Oh, she liked it. Don't listen to her." He grinned up at me. "She just doesn't want to admit that I'm right."

"Your papa is hardly ever right. You'll see when you get here."

"Now that wasn't fair," he whined, sitting up and pouting at me.

I laughed and opened my arms to him as I turned on my back. He huffed dramatically before crawling up to me and laying his head on my breast. I threaded my fingers through his hair and closed my eyes, listening to his even breathing.

"You know you and the kids are everything to me, don't you?" he whispered.

"Yes, just like you and the kids are everything to me."

He propped himself up on his elbows, leaned down, and gently kissed me again. I wrapped my arms around his neck, and we kissed languidly.

This was where I belonged. This was the life I'd dreamed of, and the man I'd dreamed of spending it with. Nothing in this world made sense until I was in his arms, and I never wanted it any other way. The past ten years hadn't always been easy, but together we'd dealt with whatever came our way, and we made it through.

Ten years ago, I counted down the days by thinking of college. Ten years ago, I hardly mattered to anyone in my school. Ten years ago, my husband made a mistake, and it brought us together no matter how hard everyone else tried to push us apart. Ten years ago, I fell in love for the first time and hadn't looked back since.

Walking through those doors tonight had proven how far I'd come— how far we'd all come. The things that I thought were most important back then had really only been minor blips on the screen. High school had helped shape me into the person that I was today, and while I wouldn't go back and do it all over again if someone paid me a million dollars, I no longer regretted or held anything against anyone.

I wasn't a famous celebrity, and I hadn't cured cancer or ended world hunger; but I was a wife to a wonderful man and a mother to a beautiful little girl and a little boy on the way. I worked hard at my job, and I loved my family. I'd say that was damn successful.